D1239719

DEPARTURE

PHILROY HINDS

For Paige Marie - In the great expanse of the universe, where space and time know no bounds, I consider myself fortunate to have shared this planet with you as a home, this generation of existence, and this lifetime in friendship with you.

PART I - PAST

I

CHANCE ENCOUNTER

June 30, 2594 saw the paratroopers of Bravo Company postured in security under the inexorable heat of Elnath, whose rays relentlessly assaulted the surface of Corina-189. Baker was an outpost under the control of Those Against and held by the 27th Infantry Brigade—the furthest of its kind from any friendly territory. As such, its main objective was to alert other posts of any movements by Those For.

Bravo had only arrived three days prior to relieve its sister Company, Alpha, after they had suffered horrible losses during an ambush. Nineteen-year-old Lieutenant Hinds and his platoon of thirty-five men and women were tasked with guarding the northern wall and serving as the "tip of the spear" in the event of an attack.

He was young for a commissioned officer, pulled early from university to fill the dwindling T.A. ranks. It had only been a year before he was assigned to lead these soldiers and placed here. Surrounding him at various positions along the wall were new soldiers, not much older than he, waiting for an enemy they had never seen. Those Against had set the least experienced troops on the frontline.

"Enemy spotted, sir! Twelve o'clock high!" one of the soldiers shouted. Hinds looked ahead of him and found half a dozen TI-84 aircraft rapidly descending on their position.

They came from nowhere, materializing immediately beneath clouds of smoke left over from an earlier bombing.

"1st Squad, fire the machine guns!" Hinds ordered. "Second Squad, get those anti-air batteries online!"

The ships approached quickly and were nearly on top of Baker before Bravo Company's remaining platoons could coordinate a response. Hinds ran to the top of the wall and peered over its edge down at the Third and Fourth squads, who he had placed outside the gate.

"Ready the turrets!" he shouted. As Third and Fourth scrambled to set up their defenses, the approaching aircraft opened their carrier bays and deployed hundreds of soldiers from the sky. Bullets tore through the air, cutting through both forces as each side defended themselves. Even against the bright sun, tracer rounds could still be seen flying across the battlefield.

Bravo Company wasn't prepared for this. Hinds ran as fast as he could toward the center of AO Baker, where the operations tent was located, and found it nearly empty upon his arrival.

"Where's the commander?" he asked. The four individuals in the room hesitated, each waiting for another to respond.

"She left this morning, sir," one of them finally said. "Went back to headquarters for a briefing with Colonel Deeley."

"What?" Hinds was shocked. *How could the commander leave without telling anyone?* he thought. "Who's in charge then?"

"Seems you are, sir."

"Go find the other PLs and send them to the north wall!" he ordered. His subordinates scrambled outside, and within minutes, the adjacent platoons were moving to reinforce the soldiers in contact with the enemy. T.F. forces were already upon them by the time they made it back, with both armies so close to one another that most of the soldiers had turned to hand-to-hand combat.

Hinds was lost in the chaos and could hardly see anything, but it was clear to him that his side would not win. Those For possessed far greater numbers, allowing them to easily break through the line. Bravo Company soldiers scrambled back toward the gate entrance, trying to avoid the barrage of gunfire from the advancing enemy line, only to be struck down by the airships still overhead.

"Fire the anti-air!" he shouted. He looked around at the towers where the batteries were placed and realized they were abandoned. Its operators had been killed, and all available replacements were trying desperately to retreat. He turned now, darting toward the closest battery with the hopes of changing their odds on his own, when suddenly a round exploded, lifting him off his feet into oblivion.

***

Hinds regained consciousness days later and found himself at an army medical station in his hometown of New Rochelle. He was alone in the commissioned officer section of the recovery room. Evidently, the other platoon leaders hadn't made it out. Hinds felt a stabbing pain in his chest as he made an effort to sit up and realized his entire torso was bandaged.

"Three broken ribs," a woman said, walking toward him. "You're among the lucky ones." He recognized the familiar voice—a woman who had treated him once after an accident during one of his earliest jumps.

"What happened?" he asked.

"You were on the wrong end of a mortar." She flipped through her notes until she got to a page with his name on it. "About a dozen of your soldiers arrived a few days ago carrying you on a makeshift litter. All of them were in bad shape."

"A dozen? Are you sure you didn't see anyone else?"

"Positive. Not a single passerby in town since."

If that was true, then he was responsible for losing the entire unit. Two-hundred and forty-nine souls had fought alongside him with no guidance, absent their commander, who had left them all to die.

"Broken ribs aren't that serious nowadays. You'll probably be back on duty soon." She moved to check on the other soldiers but stopped a few feet away and turned to face him. "Oh, a woman came by looking for you yesterday. Your commander, I think. She said you're to report to Delta Company. You've been reassigned."

He threw on his uniform and stormed out of the medical center toward Town Hall, where T.A. brass was typically known to gather. The memory of the soldiers he had left behind on the front nauseated him — they were children, wiped away from existence before their lives had even begun, and he'd never forgive himself nor his leadership for letting them down. CPT Harris owed him answers.

He arrived at a locked building, and despite ringing the buzzer multiple times, there was no answer from inside. Nearby, the parking lot adjacent to the building was filled to capacity, and Hinds knew that T.A. leadership was avoiding him, which came as no surprise. He would hide from his soldiers, too, had he run away from a fight. Irritated, he gave up and turned down the road toward *Spectator's Pub*, where he hoped to forget all that had transpired.

Spectator's was a small but fairly popular attraction, one of very few in New Rochelle. At its center was an open space where men and women danced slowly together to Vera Lynn's "We'll Meet Again." To them, the war was nothing more than a topic of conversation, something that people here spoke of but never participated in. Hinds' miserable expression, his ragged, dirty uniform, and the bandages which were clearly visible through its many tears served as an unpleasant sign of the times and caused discomfort for many as he took a seat at the bar.

"Look at the state, o'ye!" the bartender shouted with a heavy accent and a thick laugh. "Need a drink?"

"Still better looking than you, McGregor," he replied with a half-smile. "Lemme get the usual." McGregor poured him a mug of Red Stripe with foam spilling over the top. The two were good friends, as Hinds was a frequent visitor at the bar. His greeting was the same every time. "Haven't seen ye 'round the bar in at least a week. The wife keeping you?"

"Nope, just got back from Baker," Hinds replied, quickly emptying his glass.

"Aye. Heard the news all the way down here. Tough loss." McGregor passed along another mug, which was downed as swiftly as the first. Hinds' face was blank. "What's yer plan now?" the bartender asked.

"Reassignment. Makes sense after the numbers we lost."

"How many went down?"

"We left with two-hundred and fifty, returned with thirteen. Including myself."

"So many wasted lads. Was it worth it?" McGregor asked.

"We managed to hold them off a little bit. Hopefully buying T.A. time to reinforce Randall's. If they take that, there's only one stop in between T.F. and New Rochelle."

"Aye. We all need to pray then. Everything will be lost if they get here." McGregor poured himself a drink and took a seat behind the bar. "Come to think of it. There was a girl here a few nights ago saying she was being reassigned as well. Yer age, I think."

"You catch her name?"

"No, but she had the same story. Her unit was cut down at Baker, so I figured ye knew her."

"Probably came from Alpha. They were worse off than us." The two sat in silence for a while, ignoring the gossip and banter from random passersby, both keenly aware of the danger posed to their hometown. "I need something stronger."

"Aye, what d'you take me for?" He took down a bottle of Hennessy from the shelf behind him and filled a shot glass.

Hinds curled up in his seat after he drank it, hanging only faintly onto consciousness as the alcohol pulled him away from reality. "Stick to yer wine and yer beer. Yer still soft as a baby's bottom!" McGregor said. Suddenly, the doors of the bar burst open, and a woman wearing a tattered military uniform came through.

"That's the one I was tellin' ye about."

The woman sat down a few seats away from them without speaking a word to anyone around her.

"McGregor, lemme get a round for the two of us," Hinds said. The bartender was uneasy as he complied with his request.

"She's not much of a talker. Probably doesn't want botheration."

"I'll take my chances," he replied, drunk. "We need all the friends we can get these days." He took both mugs of Red Stripe, moved over to her, and placed them on the stand. "Evening, ma'am," he said.

The woman passed him nothing more than a glance from the side and returned her focus to the papers in front of her. Hinds slid a mug toward her, and she took it reluctantly. "I'm gay. Kicked the last guy in the balls for flirting with me," she said. "Just warning you."

"Don't worry. I'm taken anyway. Sort of. Just looking for company, is all. Seems like you could use some," he replied.

The woman continued to stare at him from the side while taking a sip from her drink. They sat without speaking for a while, though she did shuffle through a set of documents pulled from the assault pack on her hip. Up close, Hinds realized they were battle assessments, with the crossed-out names of soldiers killed in action.

"Are you an officer?" he asked, breaking the awkward silence.

"First Lieutenant," she replied.

"Likewise." He had her attention now, at least more of it than he previously did. "Those assessments look bad. What outfit are you with?" he asked.

"I was with Alpha Company, but they didn't make it, as I'm sure you know. You?"

"Bravo. We took your place at Baker. Sorry for your losses."

"Sorry for yours," she said. The woman signaled McGregor, who brought over more drinks for the pair. He could feel the combined weight on their shoulders as he walked away.

"You headed to Delta?" Hinds asked.

"Catching a train there tomorrow. They're a bunch of rookies on Randall's Island."

"We're all rookies out here. You don't even look like you're old enough to drink at this bar."

"You're one to talk," she replied. "What are you, twelve?"

"I'm nineteen," Hinds said. "All of my soldiers in Bravo were twenty-five or younger."

"Same. Alpha didn't have anyone over twenty." She downed her drink and requested another. Hinds followed suit.

"They're putting babies on the front," he replied, putting his head down on the bar and closing his eyes for a bit. "You gonna give me your name?"

The woman looked at him lying there but didn't say a word. Shortly afterward, Hinds passed out and remained face down at the bar.

"Cruel thing ye did there!" McGregor said to the woman, stepping over to take their drinks away from them. "Not even a name? Aye, you're breaking the man's heart!"

"He'll live," she said.

"We'll see!" He chuckled. "Soft as a cotton ball, he is!"

Two hours passed and all present in the bar returned home for the night. Hinds remained unconscious at the bar next to his new companion, who had decided to stay with him for a while. He awoke just as McGregor turned to hit the lights and call it quits until the following day. "Let's get out of here, lightweight. We have a train to catch soon," the woman said to Hinds as he struggled to sit up. He stood and immediately collapsed back onto his seat at the stand. The woman took his arm and threw it over her shoulder, and the pair proceeded toward the door. "It's Lehman, by the way. Paige Lehman."

***

The following night found the two officers at the Terminal, a network of underground cities and operations centers linked by tunnels and waterways, built in response to the rapid Those For advance. Top T.A. brass knew they would eventually lose the surface, as their enemy was just too strong and too fast. As a result, they chose to build this fortress, where T.A. could hold out until its leadership came up with an effective strategy. The Terminal expanded quickly as the exiled opponents of the Dyson Sphere took refuge behind its walls. Many of them were oblivious to the fact that this location was one of T.A's last, many of them completely unaware that their army was defeated.

The pair traveled by subway to Randall's Island, where they would receive training from their new unit, Delta Company. So far, neither of them had heard any good news about that outfit. Almost everyone there was brand new, and the formation was composed entirely of draftees and rejects from other units. Hinds and Lehman would be among the only combat veterans of the group, and so far, neither of them had seen any victories. They stood close together in the packed car, bracing themselves against one another as it shifted from side to side on the tracks. Outside, the lights that lined the walls could be seen flickering as bombing took place on the fields above.

"It's been like this every night," Lehman said. "Surprised the tunnels have held up."

"Me too," Hinds replied. "They're trying to flush us out."

"We're done if they get to us down here."

Another bomb hit the surface directly above the car, rattling the passengers down below. *Right on cue*, Hinds thought. He regained his bearing and glanced up at the car's station tracker.

"Two stops to Randall's." His counterpart remained silent. If T.F. was capable of dropping its ordinance this close to the island, the soldiers defending it probably weren't faring well.

The next ten minutes or so passed by slowly, and all aboard stood quietly until the train pulled up next to the first platform, the Terminal's entrance. Here, a large number of passengers left the car and moved toward a set of gates for in-processing. The few remaining on the subway were likely new members of Delta Company since the surface exit to Randall's Island was the next and last stop. Hinds and Lehman took seats across from one another as the car cleared. The last opportunity they would have to rest for a while.

"Where you from?" Lehman asked.

"Born and raised in New Rochelle. What about you?"

"From all over. My mother was in the military. Grew up in a town called Wurzburg."

"That's quite a ways off. Have any family around here?" Hinds asked.

"Not sure. Last I heard, they were caught in the middle of a T.F. occupation," she responded, looking down at her feet.

"I'm sorry. We'll find them."

"My family can take care of themselves, so if they're still alive, I'm not worried about them. If they aren't, then there's no sense in worrying about them," she replied. "Where's your family?"

"My mother and father passed before the war started, and my younger brother enlisted with T.A. Haven't heard from him in a while."

"You married?" Lehman continued, pointing at the ring on his left hand.

"Not sure. I had a wedding about a year ago, but my wife's parents supported the sphere, so you know what side she chose. Haven't seen or heard from her in a while either."

"Any kids?" she asked. Hinds hesitated for a moment before giving her an answer, one Lehman suspected bothered him greatly.

"She was one month pregnant when we separated." Again, both remained silent.

"We'll find them," Lehman said a while later. Hinds passed her a half-smile as the train came to a halt at its destination.

II

TYPE II

Commander Kelsey Cochran waited patiently at the Terminal's launchpad located at the facility's center. In just a few moments, she would board a shuttle that would ferry her to the *Foundation*, the interplanetary space station orbiting Elnath roughly one astronomical unit from Corina-189. The station served primarily as an observation post, monitoring the effects of the Dyson Sphere on the rest of the solar system, as the self-replicating machines it was comprised of slowly built themselves around their host star.

Cochran had spent the past week planet-side, reporting the unusual measurements recorded by her team to Colonel Deeley, the Commander of Those Against, and his subordinate leaders. The machines were replicating faster than their programming had tasked them, expanding the sphere around Elnath at a dangerous rate. Their presence seemed to be having a negative effect on the star's overall energy output—they were outpacing nuclear fusion, absorbing the energy faster than it could be produced.

The colonel didn't seem to care much, and his staff had no use for such dense information. They were so busy fighting a losing battle on the ground that they failed to acknowledge the battle they were also losing in space. The sphere's energy extraction was killing the star, and small signs were beginning to show.

And those probes…they're out of control, she thought.

Of course, no one from either side would pay attention to those problems until they were too big to fix, one of humanity's worst habits. Still, she pressed on, committed to fighting against the sphere's use in any way she could.

Cochran's thoughts were disrupted by the loud bang of the shuttle's launch mounts, all eight of which had just settled in place. They resembled the legs of a spider and were built to help the ship reach Corina-189's escape velocity without expending the vast amounts of fuel needed to make the trip.

Behind her, a technician gave the green light for her to board, and she entered a lift into its cockpit. Minutes later, she sat facing a large opening in the Terminal's ceiling, bracing herself as the shuttle prepared for takeoff.

"Launchpad prepped for departure," the technician said. "Start the main engines."

Cochran and the rest of the shuttle's crew jolted forward abruptly with their initiation.

"Lift off in fifteen…fourteen…thirteen…"

As he counted down, the commander thought of her team back on the *Foundation* and how she would explain her failure to them this time. Her three previous attempts to discuss the issue had yielded no support of any kind. He refused to give them anything.

"Nine…eight…seven…" the shuttle shook violently. Above, large pillars holding the ship vertically detached themselves and broke away. "Three…two…one…lift off!"

In seconds, the shuttle was far from the surface, ripping through the air at over thirty-thousand miles per hour, the speed necessary to escape the gravitational pull of Corina-189. The color of the sky quickly changed from blue to purple to black as the craft left the atmosphere and freed itself from 189's orbit. The dial on the speedometer steadily climbed through the numbers until the shuttle was combing the solar system at almost four million miles per hour toward mankind's furthest outpost.

The commander awoke hours later to the ship's rattling as it connected with the interplanetary space station. She unbuckled herself from her seat in the cockpit and clumsily floated to the ship's landing bay, realizing that she still couldn't get used to operating in a micro-g environment. She was met on the other end by Dr. Jorge Pajares, the resident psychologist, who had been appointed to the team to study the effects of extended space travel on mental health and behavior, but reluctantly dual-hatted as a forward-observer to study the sphere.

"How was the trip?" he asked. The two shook hands in midair.

"Long," she replied. "You'd think a Type-II civilization capable of harvesting a star would be able to travel faster."

"Well, four million miles per hour is pretty quick."

"Relatively speaking." They made their way toward a tunnel that led to the station's deck. "Four million miles is nothing in space. We'll need to go further, faster if we destroy Elnath." The pair stopped at the center of the tunnel as Jorge contemplated what she had said.

"I take it your visit to 189 didn't go well?" he asked. The commander let out a sigh and stared at the floor beneath them.

"Same as always," she said. "The war rages on, and no one is searching for a solution to the problem that's right overhead."

"That's why you're here, isn't it?"

"From here, all I can do is watch while the sphere destroys the star. Colonel Deeley won't extend any support. He thinks the issue can only be solved on the ground."

"Hm." Jorge held his chin in thought as he continued down the pathway. "Perhaps we should find someone on the ground who can convince him otherwise," he said. Cochran followed him until they arrived inside a giant glass bubble at the center of the station. This was the *Foundation*'s observation deck, from which the crew had a clear view of space in every direction.

Aside from herself and the psychologist, the room was empty, with the rest of the team likely asleep. The commander hovered to the uppermost section of the deck and looked back at Elnath. At this distance, the star appeared as a waxing gibbous, with a portion of its surface concealed by the ever-growing Dyson Sphere. The device was mankind's greatest achievement to date, allowing them to harvest the star's entire energy output.

The World Energy Association on 189 had commissioned the project years ago to counter the exhaustion of the planet's natural resources. Its design was relatively simple. It featured a shell of small, self-replicating machines that would completely surround Elnath and harvest its energy for use on 189, with eighty-percent of it sent planet-side and twenty saved by each unit for self-replication. Even T.F. was originally hesitant about its use, however, as it presented a few major obstacles.

The first was the issue of gravitation. Since the sphere would have no gravitational exchange with the star, it was liable to crash into it at random. This was remedied by a configuration of jets on each machine, which perpetually corrected their movements.

The second problem, directly related to the team's observations and routinely dismissed by leaders on the ground, was much more dire and remained unsolved. It was an issue of programming. The code behind its extraction process was faulty and occasionally caused individual units to sporadically replicate more often than they were supposed to.

The unexpected additions threw off the delicate balance of energy flow and increased the star's temperature, thus accelerating its nuclear fusion. Measurements that confirmed these findings were small but still enough to indicate the possibility that Elnath may collapse under its own weight once the sphere pushed its core to fuse carbon into iron. Should that happen to a star of this size, a resulting black hole would be imminent.

All would be lost.

The commander did her best to banish thoughts of failure from her mind. It was, after all, up to her to prevent that.

"Jorge," she said quietly. The psychologist, who was floating nearby, pulled himself along the wall and moved toward her.

"Wake the rest of the team. We're going to give this one more shot."

III

WELCOME TO DELTA

Heavy rain fell on the formation gathered at Randall's Island training area 415. The lieutenants studied everyone around them and confirmed the rumors they had heard prior to their arrival: This unit really was full of rejects. Aside from the large number of individuals who were well over the standard weight limit, there was also a handful among them wearing orange prison jumpsuits. Even convicted felons were being assigned here in desperation. There was only one other officer in the formation, another lieutenant standing in the rear.

On the wall not far in front of them was an angry captain, who seemed as excited to lead this new group as they were to follow him. More intimidating, however, was the bulky, hardened staff sergeant moving quickly up and down the ranks inspecting each of the soldiers.

"Stand at ease!" he shouted. The members of the formation placed their hands behind their backs as instructed. "My name is Staff Sergeant Adkins. Welcome to Delta Company." He paused for a long while, looking everyone in the eyes before moving on. His face was riddled with scars from conflicts past, battles that were ancient history to those who presently stood before him. He sized them up individually, silently calculating their remaining lifespans and shaking his head at each one. "Forget everything you heard before your arrival. Ignore the rumors and understand this one simple fact: Your life will not be easy here. There will be pain, there will be suffering, and there will be loss. Many of you will not survive."

He stopped pacing now and stood centered on the formation. "Behind me is your Company Commander, Captain Sullivan, a seasoned combat veteran who I've personally fought in every major battle since the start of this war. From this point on, you will follow his orders faithfully and without question. Is that understood?"

"Yes, Sergeant!" shouted the crowd in unison. SSG Adkins turned and faced the commander, who approached the group.

"Sir, they're yours." SSG Adkins rendered a salute to the commander and stepped aside.

The captain scanned the group from left to right before speaking. "Lieutenants Hinds, Lehman, and Negron, post!" he shouted. The three of them ran to the front of the formation. "You're Delta's platoon leaders. Hinds, First Platoon, Infantry. Lehman, Second Platoon, Military Police. Negron, Third, Intelligence and Reconnaissance."

The next hour was spent dividing the remaining soldiers between each platoon. Hinds was very disappointed by his lot, as he was given most of the prisoners, while the soldiers who were best suited for combat missions were allocated to Third Platoon. At the very least, he was better off than Lehman, whose entire group was overweight.

The platoon leaders were informed that Charlie Company, operating a few miles south of the island, had recently taken indirect fire from enemy scouts patrolling near their position and would likely see combat soon. CPT Sullivan estimated that it would take no more than three days for T.F. to reach their position if Charlie fell. Hinds broke through the crowd as the group was dismissed and made his way toward Lehman, who was noticeably unsettled.

"This'll be another bloodbath," she said.

"Have some faith in Charlie. They'll hold out."

"It's not Charlie I'm worried about. It's Delta. These guys are the worst of the worst. There's only one reason any army would need a unit like this."

Hinds turned and examined the soldiers once more and realized she was right. Throughout history, many wars saw the use of penal units composed of individuals just like these, and they had always served the same purpose: To act as cannon-fodder. They were bodies to be thrown at a problem and no more.

"We're gonna be sacrificed," he said.

"Exactly. CPT Sullivan knows that. If not today or tomorrow, eventually we'll be tossed away."

Before either of them could continue speaking, their attention was grabbed by SSG Adkins, who was marching quickly toward them.

"Lieutenant Hinds!" he shouted. He was the Senior Sergeant for First Platoon and second in its chain of command. "Sir, we need to get moving on a training plan ASAP. There's no time to waste."

"I'll get it done, Scottie. No worries."

SSG Adkins stormed off back toward a group of soldiers standing idly and began yelling at them.

"Guess we both have some work to do," Hinds said to his companion once Adkins had left.

"Guess so."

"I'll see you around the campfire, bud."

"I'll see you. Good luck."

They then separated in search of their platoons, now faced with the formidable task of preparing themselves for war.

***

Their first call came sooner than they had expected: Charlie Company was overrun.

Two days later, T.F. was closing in on Delta's position. CPT Sullivan watched from an observation post atop a cliff on the southern side of Randall's Island, keeping a lookout below for advancing troops. He listened carefully for footsteps, marching of any sort, but the noise of his own thoughts drowned even that of heavy rain. He knew the enemy and how they fought. Years of combat in the trenches had taught him that they did not fight fair. T.F. would catch him and his soldiers off guard, just as they always had, no matter how well Delta prepared.

Randall's Island was mostly open space with very little fortification. At its center was a small command tent surrounded by training areas of varying dimensions, built to accommodate any echelon-below-brigade-sized element that might happen to pass through them. It wasn't designed for combat and likely wouldn't even survive an attack.

The captain returned to the surface and made his way to the Island's south perimeter, where he found his soldiers in the trenches they had worked tirelessly to dig over the last few hours. First and Second Platoons were spaced evenly a few hundred meters apart and facing the Kennedy Bridge, a seemingly endless construction connecting Randall's Island to the rest of 189.

"Sir!" SSG Adkins shouted, running toward the captain. "This was the best we could do. The soldiers are standing by for your orders."

"Where is Third Platoon?" CPT Sullivan asked.

"Sir, LT Negron and his team are back at the command center monitoring movements along the bridge. We've got radio contact with them."

"Anything significant to report?"

"Only one thing, sir. T.F. has been spotted via aerial recon. They're about halfway across Kennedy and will be at our position within the hour."

"Understood. Check on the soldiers, make sure they have enough water and ammo. This will be a long one."

"Roger, sir," SSG Adkins said as he departed for the firing line.

***

Thirty minutes later, LT Hinds sat on the radio inside an impromptu bunker deep within one of the First Platoon's trenches.

"Are you there?" Hinds waited a while for an answer, hoping that Second had set up their communication systems properly. After a few seconds, a muffled response came in.

"I'm here," Lehman said on the other end.

"Are you and your guys ready?"

"No," she replied.

"Mine neither, but we'll be alright. Stay alive, and we'll get drinks afterward."

"You're buying."

Hinds smiled, though he wasn't sure that they would make it through this one. Charlie was three-hundred strong, its ranks filled with soldiers who actually knew what they were doing, yet still, T.F. defeated them quickly. Delta had nothing in the trenches but hope.

"I'll buy as many as you want. Just be safe," Hinds said. There was a long pause on the other end.

"You too. Watch your back," Lehman replied.

An alarm sounded as soon as the radios were back in their holsters, sending the soldiers of First and Second scrambling out of their rest areas over to the walls of the trenches. Hinds slowly peered over the edge to find a TI-83 mobile machine-gun bunker emplacing itself at the very end of the bridge. *They're here*, he thought. This was textbook for them, a tactic that the two officers were very familiar with. T.F. would establish a base of fire as their soldiers approached, killing anyone who rose to stop the advance.

The enemy unit was concealed behind the massive red sphere unfolding itself into a defensive position, making it impossible to guess the size of the formation that would soon make its charge. This particular TI-83 was the largest construction of its kind that the leaders of Delta had ever seen. It opened up to reveal a towering heavy cannon veiled by armor on both sides to prevent damage from enemy fire.

Hinds ran along his trench and ordered his platoon to aim their weapons just over the edge of the wall and set up a firing line. The troops inched forward carefully, knowing their heads would be swiftly removed by enemy rounds should they fail to maintain their cover. Hinds aimed his own sights toward the bridge, quietly scanning for any sign that the attack was about to start, but saw nothing. T.F. was just sitting there, waiting.

"Lehman," he said, grabbing the radio. "Do you see anything?"

"It looks like they're moving something behind the bunker, but I can't see what it is," she replied. Almost exactly on cue, the air was penetrated by sharp whistling sounds, two or three seconds apart. *Mortars*, Hinds realized.

"Everyone get down!" he shouted. *Too late.* A round exploded directly inside his trench a few hundred yards from him and another right behind First Platoon's position. The opposing force was aiming for the command center and would continue firing mortars until a round located the building. The indirect fire had to be stopped, or else the battle would be lost, but there was no way of dealing with it without first facing the machine gun.

"Scottie!" Hinds called out, trying desperately to find him in the thick cloud of dust that now surrounded Delta. It was no use. The inexperienced soldiers fled their positions, running in random directions to avoid the explosions. One after another, mortars whistled through the sky, raining death upon the scattered formation.

Then the machine gun opened fire. Red hot .50 caliber rounds ripping everyone in their way to pieces. Left and right, bodies were tossed around the battlefield, and there was nowhere to hide.

Hinds jumped up and darted across the line to Second Platoon, where Lehman was returning fire from her bunker.

"This is bad!" she screamed.

"Yeah, but it could be worse!" Hinds replied. He was technically correct. This battle hadn't witnessed an offensive from any sort of aircraft, which was more of a surprise to him than anything else, considering his last engagement with T.F.

"We need to take out that MG!" Lehman shouted.

"I know! Do you have a plan?"

"No! Do you?"

"I say we go over the top and rush it!" Hinds declared. "We stay here. We're dead anyway!"

Lehman stopped firing and stared at him in shock. The plan was suicide. They were separated from the gun by more than three-hundred meters of open space. Under these conditions, that was infinity—anything was more likely than success. Even if they did manage to make it across the field and take out the gun, they would be left to deal with the assembly of enemy troops gathered behind it. Alone.

"I need you to trust me!" he shouted. "We can reach it!"

"That's a stupid plan, Hinds!"

"But it's the right one!" Lehman wasn't sure if he was brave or genuinely crazy, but she trusted him.

The dust was so thick at this point that the pair had trouble seeing one another. The mortar fire was picking up, increasing in intensity and speed, leveling Delta's position. Their defenses were reduced to almost nothing. All that was left now was this one trench, this single line of bunkers to protect anyone who could reach it from the danger above.

Suddenly, out of the corner of his eye, Hinds spotted SSG Adkins racing through the cloud toward their position, rattled but uninjured.

"Lieutenant Hinds!" he shouted, staying low to avoid the hail of bullets flying overhead.

"Aye, Scottie!" Hinds said, leaving his position to greet him.

"Sir, ma'am, we're pinned down! The soldiers can't move without getting blown away!" More bullets flew past him as he spoke.

"We're tracking. There's a machine gun set up about three-hundred yards that way!" Hinds pulled him over to their position at the wall to keep from being hit. The group could hear soldiers being cut down and screaming in pain outside.

"We need to do something before we're all killed here!"

"We've got a plan, Sarge!" Hinds shouted. "We'll go over the top and take out the gun! When it's down, I need you to move the remaining soldiers up to our position as fast as you can!"

Before he could respond, the lieutenants grabbed their weapons and prepared to move.

"You with me, Mama?" Hinds asked.

"I'm with you!"

Side by side, the pair stepped forward, climbed over the top of the wall, and ran together into the devastating fire.

"Damn!" Hinds shouted, gritting his teeth. A round clipped him in the arm the moment he stepped over. *Not a .50 cal*, he thought, that would have taken his arm off. Instead, it was a smaller round. 5.56? Perhaps. If that were true, then there was a new problem: That bullet didn't come from the MG. It came from the soldiers behind it. They were making their charge.

"Lehman!"

"I know!" She watched them emerge from the structure like bees from a hive.

Seventy-five meters in, the pair continued their advance, feeling infinitely far from both sides as they traded the relative safety of the trench for a wide-open field and ran toward the enemy. Seconds passed slowly, and Hinds could see the fire concentrating on their position, tracer rounds burning hot as they flew close by. Then, out of nowhere, a mortar exploded, hurling them back and covering them in dust.

Stupid plan, Hinds thought, second-guessing himself as he tried to pull himself up. They were separated now, and he couldn't find Lehman in the cloud, nor could he tell what direction he was facing.

Roughly thirty seconds passed as he waited for the dust to settle, keeping as low as he possibly could in the open. How he hadn't been struck down by the gunfire all around him or killed by the mortar was a miracle. He wondered whether his companion was as fortunate. Fortune, however, was not with him when the air began to clear. Ahead, less than one-hundred meters away, was a battalion-sized element of T.F. soldiers, four times the size of Delta, at least. Hinds scanned the area once more but still found no sign of Lehman.

Taken by the blast, he thought. *Nothing left to lose now.*

He figured things always went this way, or at least they had throughout the war. Every time he cared about someone, even just a little bit, they disappeared. This loss, for him, was the last straw. Facing the advance, Hinds fixed a combat knife to the end of his rifle, loaded his weapons, and charged against them alone.

***

CPT Sullivan leaned against the wall of Kennedy Bridge with SSG Adkins and the remaining soldiers of Delta Company. They stood forty strong, a small fraction of the formation that began the defense only hours earlier but still large enough for a counterattack. LT Negron, who was back at the command center, realized that T.F. had completely focused their fire on Hinds and Lehman, opening up a route along their western flank that the rest of Delta could use to regroup without being detected. For all they knew, T.F. Still thought they were rushing toward wounded soldiers in the trenches, but they were wrong.

The plan was simple now. Once the last of the enemy soldiers filtered through from behind the TI-83, CPT Sullivan would lead his own assault and attack the unsuspecting troops from the rear, and he would do it with their own weapon, the MG atop the bunker. He would hold that position and eliminate as many of them as possible, leaving his small team to take out the rest. He just needed his platoon leaders to continue causing enough disturbance to provoke the enemy out onto the battlefield, so he could reach the gun.

Initially, he had planned on occupying the MG by force, but upon their arrival at the structure realized that all possible openings, save for the one T.F. used for their assault, were too narrow to move groups through. Had they tried, they would have been picked off a few at a time. Stealth and deception were the only options left, and it was up to Hinds and Lehman to distract their enemy for as long as was necessary.

"Negron, this is CPT Sullivan," he said over a radio message to the command center, "Do you have a visual on the other PLs?"

"Negative, sir," he replied, concerned. His place in line during Delta's first formation was the only thing that kept him off the battlefield today. Had he been chosen to lead First or Second, he would be out there now, overrun by the enemy.

"No visual on either, sir," he continued. "But the enemy is pinpointing at one location."

They're still fighting. CPT Sullivan handed the radio to SSG Adkins, pulled his binoculars from a pouch on his vest, and held them to his eyes for a better view of the combat a hundred meters away. This technology was ancient. In an age where mankind was harvesting stars, he figured they would at least equip him and his troops with something better than standard-issue equipment.

Through his antiquated optics, he found the pinpointed area of the battle and saw LT Hinds pushing back against T.F. in close quarters, fighting most of them hand to hand. Lehman was not with him. Scanning further south, about fifty meters back, he found her lying in a crater opened up by a mortar blast. The faint rise and fall of her chest indicated that she was breathing and alive. She was shielded from the terror above by the angle of the pit she was in and hidden from view, kept safe from the enemy by her companion, who probably didn't even know she was alright.

CPT Sullivan needed to make his move now, or neither of them would survive. When the last of T.F. trickled past the wall, Sullivan ran inside the structure and climbed up to the controls of the MG.

***

Hinds was able to pick off T.F. soldiers with ease. Their army depended almost entirely upon long-range weapons systems and giant formations to overwhelm their adversaries before they had a chance to fight back. This terrain, however, did not create the ideal conditions for their usual tactics.

First, the mortars they fired picked up incredible amounts of dust, which concealed First and Second from the heavy machine-gun fire. Then, T.F. soldiers had to run out from behind the TI-83 in small groups because the fortification was so large that it only left narrow openings between its walls and the sides of the bridge. They never regrouped once they were in the field, and their failure to do so brought them to Hinds in teams of two or three.

Finally, their advanced, high-powered rifles were not designed to function efficiently in close quarters, and these soldiers were not skilled in hand-to-hand combat. They figured there was no need for them to be. Not with weapons like those, not against an untrained force like this.

Out of ammo and injured, Hinds pressed on, cutting down the enemy one at a time until he heard the harsh grinding of the MG. Not again. He spun around and quickly ran toward the nearest impact crater, diving inside just before the gun let off its rounds.

"Lehman!" he shouted.

There she was, covered in blood and seriously wounded at the bottom of the pit, but alive. She gave no response, nor did she even acknowledge that he was there. He examined her head, ensuring there were no signs of trauma, then inspected and applied bandages to her wounds. She was in shock. The mortar blast sent large pieces of shrapnel into her chest and abdomen, and she was bleeding profusely.

"I've gotta get you out of here." Hinds leaned over the edge of the crater and found the command center. He would have to carry her under fire over the entire distance they had crossed before in order to get her help. Looking back toward the bridge, he noticed that the opposing army was no longer advancing on their position. *They're running away.* The MG was firing down at T.F.

***

"Give 'em hell, sir!" SSG Adkins shouted as he watched CPT Sullivan on the gun. The plan was working. Enemy soldiers were caught completely off guard. Sullivan shifted the gun horizontally along the battlefield, pushing T.F. away from his lieutenants. Through his optics, SSG Adkins saw Hinds carrying Lehman back toward the command center.

"Spread out along the flank!" CPT Sullivan ordered, indifferent to the carnage beneath him, the torrent of bodies collapsing to the ground by his hand as he pushed his sights further — he intended to drive the survivors right into his formation.

Delta Company soldiers formed a thin line across the western flank and fired their weapons perpendicular to the MG. The enemy was caught in a hail of bullets from both directions and left with nowhere to run. Within seconds it was over, and Randall's Island was quiet. T.A. had won. The battalion that had arrived hours earlier was strewn out across the open field, defeated by a small company of ragtag soldiers. T.F. would not take this lightly, and a swift retaliation was almost guaranteed, but for now, CPT Sullivan was satisfied. The war had yielded a great number of major losses and only a few minor victories for T.A. Perhaps the rest of the force would view this as a reminder that there was still a fighting chance.

There was still hope.

IV

NEGOTIATIONS

Days later, CDR Cochran and Dr. Pajares waited aboard a shuttle hurtling through 189's atmosphere back toward the surface. The commander had developed a plan that she hoped would convince Colonel Deeley to lend her team support.

If all went favorably, they could secure the resources they needed to prepare the planet for the myriad of worst-case scenarios tendered by the Dyson Sphere. Or at least some of them. There was an infinite number of things that might go wrong with mankind's project based on the readings taken from the space station, and only so much could be done to avert them.

The ship struggled against the turbulence of the atmospheric drag, shaking its passengers violently in their seats. It wasn't the most aerodynamic of crafts, still sporting a bulky design similar to space shuttles of old. They owed this experience to the lack of technological evolution over the last few centuries—funds for research and development of space travel were often cast away on meaningless projects.

Cochran reflected on the delays in R&D that would cost them, realizing that the butterfly effect of past decisions would require her team to make major breakthroughs on every front to mitigate their present concerns. She thought of the Differential Sail, a device that allowed forward propulsion of spacecraft at a third of the normal expenditure of fuel, initially introduced a millennium prior.

At the time of its inception, now-defunct political parties were more concerned with funding the exploration and conquest of then-dead planets. Resources were poured into the establishment of useless military posts, dissuading expenditure on new technologies. As a result, the Differential Sail was abandoned and wouldn't be reintroduced again for more than five-hundred years. When it was, society rallied for a time to test long-distance space travel, but only briefly before the implosion of 189's economy. The subsequent conflict once again eclipsed the development of useful advancements.

With funding slashed almost entirely, mankind settled for the launch of a single project—the Huguenot I, a seed ship stocked with samples of human, animal, and plant DNA dispatched to a nearby star system as a primitive form of interstellar colonization.

After only a few years, the focus was shifted away from its journey and eventually discarded, as teams on the ground lost track of its progress and location. Kelsey rolled her eyes at the thought of the latter project, certain that the money spent on it would have been better utilized studying more comfortable forms of atmospheric reentry.

The shuttle descended quickly through 189's mesosphere, lending relief from the turbulence that its passengers had endured for the last ten minutes. After only a short while, the pair was hanging just a few thousand feet above the Terminal. Through the clouds, Cochran could see the structure, a large dome that was used to conceal and protect The *Foundation*'s launchpad. Beneath it was a labyrinth of tunnels that connected every resource, facility, and town under T.A's control. As she drew closer, the commander observed deep craters along the wall of the dome, covering most of its surface.

"From the bombings," Jorge said, tightening his harness as they prepared to land.

"Those haven't let up at all. Not one bit," Cochran replied. She studied the landscape around the perimeter of the dome and noticed the same craters spread out over a distance of what must have been hundreds of miles. "This is the only thing standing in between them and victory. Destroy these connections, and our soldiers will be cut off from one another."

"I'm surprised it's still here, after all the damage they've already done." The Terminal's underground wasn't exactly a secret, thanks to the many T.A. defectors who ran to the winning side. Thousands of bombing missions had been carried out by T.F. commanders hoping to eliminate the final stronghold and become war heroes. It was only a matter of time before one of them actually did.

The commander deployed the ship's parachutes and decreased their speed enough to allow the landing bay harness to catch them as they arrived at their destination. The landing, at least, was smooth, owing to the "blanket" harness that enabled faster reentry. Cochran gave a sigh of relief as they touched down one more time successfully. Every departure and reentry they made without being blown out of the sky by T.F. was a miracle.

"Ready to go?" Dr. Pajares asked.

"As ready as I'll ever be."

Colonel Deeley would be waiting for them inside with the rest of the command staff gathered at Central Terminal. Cochran had chosen this day for that very reason, the colonel on his own would quickly dismiss her proposal, but the rest of them would listen. She was sure of it.

The pair left the shuttle and proceeded down a decompression tube at the far corner of the landing bay, serving as an elevator that lowered them down to the Terminal's platform. It was empty, save for the railcar operators, air traffic controllers, and some janitorial staff. At this point in the afternoon, everyone that mattered to the *Foundation*'s team was probably hidden away in some meeting.

"We're a little late," Cochran said, looking down at her watch. The time was 16:15, thirty minutes after the scheduled start of their engagement.

"We'll blame it on a rough landing," Jorge replied.

The pair picked up their pace and made haste for the colonel's chambers. Cochran felt her feet dragging more and more with each step as her confidence slowly left her. She wasn't sure this plan would work, given COL Deeley's stubbornness and the subject matter of her most recent proposal. This time, she had to convince him there was no point in continuing the war.

They arrived at the Warren, an expansive system of hallways built like a maze on the lower levels of the Terminal, used to disorient and trap unsuspecting intruders. Its walls were lined with numbered doors that led to nowhere in particular.

Rooms of varying sizes, most of which were completely empty, others were furnished to present a false image of significance to an outsider. All of them were meaningless.

Many T.F. operatives had learned the hard way, losing themselves forever in the seemingly endless structure.

Terminal employees, on the other hand, had a simple way through the labyrinth. At Warren's entrance was a panel with a switch that controlled the lights for the room. Underneath the panel was a keypad where users could enter specific codes which would light the appropriate paths to their destinations. There were only four offices on the other end of the maze.

However, the codes changed every day, so entering random numbers was pointless and incorrect codes would light the entire room, providing no guidance whatsoever. Cochran drew a breath, hoping the colonel hadn't changed the code to his quarters at the last moment in order to keep her from showing up. Gently, she lifted the panel and began typing:

5-7-5-2

Cochran waited a moment for the familiar click, breathing a sigh of relief as the lights above flickered on, tracing a path through the halls. She followed it, moving faster now as her anticipation grew, reaching the colonel's chambers within minutes. The pair entered to find that a meeting had already begun. Prestigious members from both the civilian and military sectors of T.A. were seated around an oval-shaped booth that was almost large enough to fill the room.

At its center was Colonel Dennis Deeley, Commander of Those Against, sitting proudly in his military dress uniform. His chest was lined with awards, medals from long past and forgotten campaigns, symbols of both meritorious service and old age. He was intimidating as always.

Colonel Deeley's eyes settled on the scientists when they walked in, bringing the discussion in the room to an end. On his desk in front of him, a small machine whistled quietly, flashing images quickly across its screen. Cochran was thankful for the tiny hum. It was the only distraction from the heavy silence resting on her shoulders as she waited for the colonel to speak.

It was a UNIVAC 5000, an advanced computer that enabled the transmission of 360-degree battle-space projections, allowing senior commanders to make decisions in real-time. Cochran had heard that technology was still in development by T.F. It was rumored to be their so-called "secret weapon" that would end the war in their favor. She had never expected to see it completed, let alone in the hands of T.A.

"We're not as hopeless as you think, Kelsey," he said.

CDR Cochran stood frozen, anticipating the check-mate that was headed her way. Colonel Deeley rose to his feet and switched on the UNIVAC's projector, filling the space inside the oval booth with a holographic image of Corina-189 and the objects suspended in its orbit. He waved his hand, prompting the image to zoom in toward the planet's northern hemisphere, and closed his fist, ordering the device to stop. The hologram was centered on the streets of a large city, which were lined with soldiers on both sides engaged in intense combat.

"We have the ability to see ahead, to predict the enemy's movements and stay one step in front of them." the colonel continued, waving his hand again and focusing the hologram on military aircraft that hovered in the sky above the city. Hundreds of TI-84's dangled in the air, surrounded by a seemingly equal number of outdated T.A. fighter jets swarming around them like flies. "The element of surprise is no longer an asset to Those For. The 5000 lets us see it all...combat across the five dimensions of warfare: Land, sea, air, space, and cyberspace."

He put both hands together now and separated them, panning the image out to the area thousands of feet above the city, where a T.A. laser satellite was positioned and ready to rain death down upon the enemy birds. "If utilized correctly by my subordinate commanders, we will win this war. Sooner than we had ever thought."

Brief applause echoed throughout the quarters as the colonel roused his clan of aristocrats. Cochran's face flared red from anxiety. She was about to question his authority and resolve with an argument that seemed far less valid now after his display.

"But still not soon enough," she interjected. Cochran held her breath, approached the projection, and repeated the same motion with her hands as Colonel Deeley had done before, hoping desperately that it would work the same way. The image zoomed even further out to the absolute limit of the 5000, displaying the three planets closest to Elnath. She pointed at the shell, which engulfed all but just a tiny crescent-shaped section of the star.

"You're out of time, Colonel. The drones are still projected to destroy our star, regardless of the outcomes of this conflict. Those For played us all for fools, using the war as a distraction to buy their creation more time to grow, and you couldn't see that even with your advanced technology." She paused momentarily, looking back at Jorge, whose expression suggested she had overstepped an inch too far.

This is it, she thought.

"Sir, it's true that the 5000 can help us wage war at levels beyond human understanding, but it doesn't solve the real problem, the greatest issue mankind has ever faced. We're going to lose our star, and those drones won't go out quietly. The death of Elnath will be catastrophic for the entire system.

"We're all aware of that, Kelsey," the Colonel cut in. "Hence why Those Against exists in the first place and why we must continue to fight relentlessly, despite your opposition. Would you have us just give up and let them complete their project without resistance?"

"Sir, you're not listening. We're past the point of no return. Elnath is finished regardless of who wins or loses. It's time for us to run. It's time for all of us to run."

V

FAITH

Lehman came to her senses nine days after the Battle for Randall's Island. She woke slowly to the familiar surroundings of Sound Shore Medical Camp, a civilian treatment facility in New Rochelle located near a cliff overlooking the ocean. Staring out the plastic window of her tent, she saw nurses walking swiftly from one area of the camp to another, inspecting other wounded patients. They were likely all soldiers from Delta carried in after the fight. She studied the nurses' expressions, searching for signs of worry or dismay, but found none. They were calm, despite their unusual hurry. She turned away from the window and inspected her own injuries. Her torso was wrapped in bandages, red with recently dried blood.

"Broken ribs. Lot of folks coming through here with those lately," a woman said, approaching her. "Not much they can do about it. Good to see you're finally awake, though." She stopped a few inches away from Lehman's cot, looking down at her. Lehman was momentarily caught in a trance, admiring the stranger in front of her. A handsome woman about the same age as she, with beautiful eyes and a smile she found rather angelic. "I'm Captain Ryan Cortese, a pilot with the 27th Aviation Battalion, Those Against. I flew you here."

The lieutenant attempted to sit up straight out of respect for the higher rank. Her uniform was unfamiliar, giving very little indication that she was military. T.A. had so few pilots that it was rare for soldiers to ever meet one in person.

"What happened out there?"

"Well, it seems you guys won," CPT Cortese said. "You Delta soldiers are something else."

Lehman turned toward the window again and observed the scene outside. The last thing she remembered was charging out into the fray under withering fire. As far as she was concerned, she should not have survived.

"One of them carried you to the extraction point all by himself," the captain continued.

Lehman didn't respond. Images from the battle flashed through her mind. She remembered tracer rounds flying by her head as their bright streaks filled the sky. She remembered the violent quakes they endured as mortars struck the ground near them and the many times they narrowly escaped death. Then her memories went black, and all she could think of was her friend standing there on his own as hundreds of T.F. soldiers charged his position. She shook her head and stood, throwing her uniform on in one fluid motion, guilt-ridden for letting him fight alone.

"Need a drink?"

"Something strong," Lehman replied.

"It's a long walk to Spec's. I'll join you."

"No thanks." She looked up at her just in time to catch her smile fading away.

The wind blowing through the room sent loose strands of hair from the captain's bun, and she brushed her hand across her head to set them back in place. She was hurt, but she hid it well, and Lehman found that beautiful.

"Maybe next time," she continued impulsively, taking care not to push her away.

"Next time."

***

Spectator's was unusually full for this time of day. Mid-afternoon never saw a party like this, but the recent victory against T.F. had the town running wild even a week later. News of the battle filled every screen in the bar and the conversation at every table. The soldiers, at least the ones who made it back unharmed, boasted of their daring feats and triumphs in combat to their civilian friends. Glasses were emptied all around as the locals celebrated a step forward with one another.

Hinds sat alone in a booth at the far end of the room, listening to the smooth whistle of the horns in Glenn Miller's "Moonlight Serenade" playing softly in the background amidst the noise. He was a hero to the crowd, having spent most of the last few days hailed in the papers as the "lone warrior" who "held destiny and fate in his hands," though he knew he hadn't done anything special.

To him, his actions weren't significant. He simply did what anyone in the same situation would have. It wasn't as though he had many choices in the matter. Either fight or stand there and die. With options like that, what else could he have done? The real details of the fight lingered in his mind—the details without an eye-witness alive to share them. All he could think about was his soldiers. He hadn't gotten to know them very well, but he knew for sure that there were good men and women out there who deserved to come home, and they didn't.

Then there was Lehman. He never went to go see her after the pilot flew her away, haunted by the memory of her slung over his wounded shoulder, unconscious and bleeding.

"Aye, ye look like ye been hit by another mortar!" McGregor proclaimed, cheerful as always. The bartender took a seat at the booth and poured the two of them a drink.

"That's been happening a lot these days."

"Don't know whether yer luck is good or bad! Either bad that ye've been hit or good that ye made it out!" The pair clinked their glasses together and emptied them. "Oy! That was a strong one!" he shouted. "I call that one 'Fool's Charge', 'named in honor of ye and yer lass! Heard all about ye's from the townsfolk. Risky plan, don't ye think?"

"But it worked, didn't it?"

"Ye'll never see thirty if ye keep actin 'like that! How old is ye anyhow?"

"Nineteen."

"Oy! Not even old enough t'drink! I ought to tell yer mother. God bless 'er soul! She'd beat that dark skin right off ye if she knew! Aye, she'd beat me for servin 'ye!"

"I think I've earned these."

"Can't argue wi 'that!" McGregor let out a loud belch and leaned back in his seat. Behind him, Hinds saw the doors at the entrance fly open. It was Lehman. He watched her walk across the room, unnoticed by the rest of the crowd, blood still stained across the uniform she wore the day of the battle.

She covered down on the only remaining seat at the bar, a little corner stool that sat near the jukebox, and said nothing to anyone.

"Aye…there she is, lad. Go talk to 'er," McGregor said, catching his stare. "I'm sure she'll be happy to see ye."

"She's never happy," Hinds replied. He continued to watch her and debated whether or not he should. She had almost died because of his plan, and he would rather not have to answer for that. "I think I'll pass."

"In life, ye have to seize the opportunity, boy. Do ye think ye'll get the chance to save her life again? Seize the opportunity."

"You've had too many, Chief. What are you talking about?"

"Ye know wha 'I'm sayin. Why'd ye do it? That's wha ' I'm talkin 'about." His speech faded into a slur of mumbled nonsense, and he passed out, falling flat over the table and knocking his glass to the floor.

The room paused when it shattered, and everyone left their own little worlds to observe the commotion, but only for a moment. The old bartender usually ended his day like this, with a glass too many and some unintelligible words of wisdom, so no one paid him any mind. Hinds returned his focus to Lehman, who was already staring at him from across the room when he looked up, the noise having compromised his position.

"No hiding now," Hinds said. He drew a deep breath and walked toward her, subconsciously judging the distance between himself and the door as he made his approach. *Why'd he do it? Seize the opportunity? What the hell was he talking about?* he thought.

His mind raced, flashing back and forth between thoughts of what to say to Lehman And images of her laying in the crater after the explosion. He arrived at the bar and met her gaze again, her sea-foam eyes brilliant and fierce under Spectator's ambient light, and suddenly, his questions were answered. He knew why he did it, why he was able to stand fearless against a horde of enemy soldiers to protect her and where he got the strength to carry her miles away to safety after the fight. He loved her, and he couldn't let her go.

The pair stared at one another for a while, both waiting in silence for the other to speak. The room seemed to go silent then, and the crowd dancing around them slowly faded away into nothing.

"Lehman, I—"

"Don't expect me to thank you," she interrupted. "It was your stupid plan that put us there in the first place." Lehman turned her back to him and faced the screen across the bar.

"Glad you're okay," Hinds replied. He waited a moment, hoping she had something more to say, and turned to leave when she didn't. The crowd parted almost empathetically as he passed them by.

"Glad you're okay too," Lehman whispered. She took a large sip from her glass as the jukebox repeated its cycle, and Vera Lynn's "We'll Meet Again" began playing overhead.

It would be a long war.

***

The return trip to Delta that night was terrible. T.F. artillery struck the surface directly above the underground railroad every thirty seconds or so, shaking the train and occasionally knocking standing passengers off their feet. Outside the car, the tunnel lights flickered as they passed and debris from its walls trickled down like thick snow with each shell that made contact. The attacks slowed their pace significantly, keeping the train below twenty miles per hour the entire way in order to avoid an accident with any debris that may have fallen onto the tracks. It was like this every time. Veteran passengers were all too familiar with the relentless barrage of enemy rounds.

Hinds sat toward the rear of the car, holding his head in his hands as he struggled to fight the headache and nausea caused by excessive drinking earlier on. Before falling asleep, he had consumed more than a bottle of wine back in his quarters, and it was quickly catching up to him. The unsteady rocking of the train was not supportive of his well-being, and he felt the contents of his stomach moving upwards into his chest.

On his left was a man who looked to be in his fifties, reading a copy of the local newspaper Talk of the Sound and occasionally snickering at the stories inside.

"Did you see this?" he asked. Hinds looked up at him, unsure of who he was speaking to since his face was still buried in the paper, and gave no response. The man continued anyway. "There's an article on page seven about the Dyson Sphere. It's growing more unstable by the day." He poked his head out from behind the newspaper and looked down at the young man. The lenses of his spectacles were thick, making his eyes appear much larger than they really were.

"I wouldn't know much about that, sir," Hinds replied.

"About the sphere? Isn't that why you're fighting? You're a soldier, aren't you?" He flipped to a different section of the paper and handed it to Hinds. "There's an article about you right here." It was a story about the battle on Randall's Island, with a small picture of his face printed at the very top of the page. The lieutenant turned away and faced the floor of the car. After a few long seconds without a response, the man returned to his paper and continued flipping through the pages. "I'm Anirban, by the way. Anirban Acharya. I'm a researcher at Central Terminal."

"Pleased to meet you," Hinds replied sarcastically, nearly stumbling out of his seat as the tunnel shook against the incoming blasts.

"We have nowhere to go after this," the man said, fixing his glasses. "Those For can fight for their sphere all they want, but it won't change the facts. If those drones continue replicating out of control, 189 will be lost, and there's nowhere else to go."

The train screeched to a halt as it arrived at its second stop and Anirban's final destination: Central Terminal. Sliding doors on the opposite side of the car opened, and passengers squeezed their way through. The man rose to his feet, folded his paper, and placed it on the seat below.

"Take care of yourself, young man, and never lose sight of the real issues at hand." Anirban disappeared into the crowd and the car doors shut as the train continued along.

Hinds leaned his head back into his hands and saw a picture in the newspaper on the seat beside him. It was a picture of Elnath, 189's host star, nearly encapsulated by the growing Dyson Sphere. All that could be seen of it was a crescent-shaped sliver of light, an area that would soon be covered up when the project was completed. The man had undoubtedly left that for him on purpose, perhaps expecting him to do something about it.

Civilians, he thought, disappointed at Anirban's apparent ignorance.

Had he understood the conflict, he would know that there was nothing a low-ranking officer could do about anything. Hinds looked down at the rank insignia on his chest—a black bar, one of the most junior ranks among commissioned officers, a small fish in an ocean of sharks. It would never be his responsibility to address the issue, never at his level, with the little experience he had.

At any rate, no one had done anything about it anyway, at least not openly. Government officials who stood in opposition to the project insisted on throwing all of their available resources behind the war, and judging by the structure presented in the image, it was clear their effort was in vain. The sphere continued to grow regardless of how much fighting was done on 189—the war was simply a distraction.

That was the real problem. All of the suffering T.A. had gone through, all the losses they would continue to take as the fighting dragged on, meant nothing, not if they couldn't stop the growth of the sphere.

The train pulled into its final stop, the underground gate at Randall's Island, and opened its doors for the few remaining passengers aboard. Hinds remained seated, watching the last of them go, clutching the image tightly in his hands as the doors closed again and the train started off back toward Central Terminal.

***

Lehman gripped the belt of her harness tightly as the helicopter leaped into the air and away from New Rochelle. CPT Cortese had offered her a ride back to Randall's Island by way of air travel, promising smoother passage than the underground train. So far, her word was questionable. The aircraft ascended rapidly, and within minutes, the crew was hundreds of feet above the city. Lehman looked out over the edge and was just able to catch the city hall clock tower receding in the distance, its large hands illuminated by the lights surrounding the clock's base. It was the only thing she could see this high up at night.

They chose to fly once Elnath had set in order to avoid detection by TI-84s patrolling the area. T.F. aircraft couldn't see very well in darkness, which gave T.A. one of their very few advantages since these days 'darkness came more frequently.

"Damned fools!" CPT Cortese shouted. Lehman could barely hear her over the tremor of the helicopter's wings. "I guess they didn't realize covering up the star would dim the lights!" Daytime was about four hours shorter than it had been before the construction began, and it was almost fascinating that no one anticipated a solution to that problem or even seemed to care about it at all.

"Works out well for us!" the co-pilot shouted. She was a Specialist whose name Lehman couldn't remember. Next to her manning the railgun on the helicopter's right side was another Specialist of the same age, Beedy, she thought his name was. They were babies. She wasn't much older, but she still felt for them. They shouldn't be out here.

"You're awful quiet, LT!" Lehman looked up toward the cockpit of the aircraft and found CPT Cortese staring back at her, hands still tightly gripping the bird's controls as she commanded it to climb. "Nervous about going back?" Lehman hesitated for a moment and realized that all eyes were now on her.

"Not at all, ma'am," she replied, turning away.

Truthfully, she wasn't nervous. Randall's Island didn't scare her, nor was it the location of her worst day in the military. She thought back to her time with Alpha Company, where she spent a year running detainee operations at AO Baker. Her team of eight soldiers was responsible for overseeing hundreds of T.F. prisoners, all held inside an open camp with very little security. They had managed to keep them under control, preventing any significant mishaps for months, then on one quiet morning when nothing seemed out of the ordinary, TI-84's filled the skies, and the bombings started.

A year without action riddled Alpha with complacency, and the entire company was caught off guard when the attack began. The lieutenant found herself in a particularly bad situation that day when all of the prisoners rushed the entry control point simultaneously the moment the alert sounded, as though they had known the attack was coming all along. Sentries at the gates, only armed with non-lethal weapons, were overwhelmed immediately, and within seconds, the detainees were free.

Lehman watched the event unfold from behind the glass panes of the prison control room and stood in awe as the riot headed her way. She was alone, her entire team taken out by the crowd and no one available to lend aid since everyone else was by this time either killed or occupied in fighting elsewhere. They reached her position quickly and used anything they could get ahold of to break down the doors and smash the glass panes.

Just as they managed to break through, they were engulfed in a bright flash of light, and then suddenly, everything went black.

Lehman woke hours later, covered by a large pile of debris and surrounded by the dismembered bodies of the prisoners that had tried to escape. She remembered spending what seemed like an eternity digging herself out of the mess, just to find that she was the only remaining soldier from Alpha, the only one who survived the attack.

After that, there was nothing that could make her nervous. What bothered her now was her last conversation with her rescuer, who she had abandoned twice.

"Good to hear!" the captain shouted, snatching Lehman away from her unpleasant thoughts.

Two hours went by quietly as the crew continued to push forward toward Randall's Island. Lehman switched seats with the co-pilot, and both specialists moved into the cabin to rest while they flew through friendly airspace.

"Take a look at that," CPT Cortese said, pointing a finger at the domed structure beneath them. It was the Terminal.

Lehman hadn't seen it up close before and never from above. The towering beast was illuminated all around by blue lights spotting its surface to alert nearby aircraft.

"Isn't it something?" The captain flipped the transponder switch on the control panel, signaling friendly air-defense assets on the ground not to fire, then set the helicopter to autopilot, directing it on a course around the

Terminal. Lehman watched in fascination as they slowly circled the dome, passing so close to its surface that she thought they might collide.

"Yeah, it's something." She looked over her shoulder at CPT Cortese, who had leaned back in her seat with her feet on the control panel and her eyes closed. She was brilliant under the blue light passing through the cockpit. Lehman waited a moment, then moved toward her and kissed her gently. She was caught off guard by her mutual exchange. The captain opened her eyes and stared at her, expression relaxed as though the kiss was expected.

"I apologize, ma'am," Lehman said.

"You can call me Ryan," she replied, smiling. Ryan took her hand, and the pair watched as the craft lifted away from the Terminal and ascended through the clouds.

Hinds forced his way aimlessly through the crowd at Central Terminal, scanning the area in search of Anirban Acharya. He had managed to lose the old man completely in the fifteen minutes it took for the train to return to this stop from Randall's Island. The space inside was narrow and filled with people pushing past one another so violently that it was a miracle no one fell onto the tracks below. They were all headed toward a single set of stairs at the center of the room, which led to the upper levels of the Terminal. Hinds advanced with the group up the stairs and arrived at a map hanging from a wall in the center of the path that divided it in three.

"You are here," he said quietly, tracing his finger from the red dot marking his location down each of the three paths. The hallway on the left ended at a large research facility, most likely where the old man would be, given his occupation on the Terminal. It was also the only direction that no one else was going. The crowd continued to funnel past Hinds down the central and rightmost path. He broke away from the group and proceeded to the left alone, looking over his shoulder every few seconds to ensure he hadn't drawn any unwanted attention.

Fifteen minutes later, he found himself shuffling through a featureless labyrinthine structure with closed doors lining its walls and no one in sight. He wandered aimlessly from one hallway to the next, each turn leading him nowhere.

"What the hell is this?" Hinds sat against the wall, his head still pounding fiercely, and the bright lights overhead made it difficult to concentrate. He shielded his eyes and looked up at the ceiling to find that most of the lights in the room were out, save for a singular line of panels that seemed to trace a path across the room. He followed them, quickly cutting through the maze and arriving at a set of doors left slightly ajar by the room's occupants ahead. He leaned his head against the opening and listened to the faint sound of an argument coming from inside.

"We need to consider the Drive, sir. It's our best, and perhaps only, option," a woman said.

"You're willing to bet our future on an experiment? The Drive is hypothetical nonsense. It won't work," came another voice, which Hinds didn't recognize. He peered around the edge of the door, maintaining a low profile as best he could.

Beyond stood a pair of officers, both wearing unfamiliar uniforms, speaking to a man Hinds had seen in the papers before. It was Colonel Deeley, Commander of Those Against.

On his right was Anirban Acharya, stoically observing the discussion in front of him.

How is he here? Hinds thought, unsure of how a researcher could be in the same league as someone of such high rank.

"Even if we could build one, the resources required to construct it don't exist," the colonel continued.

"That's not true. They exist. We just need to secure them."

"Humor me, Kelsey. Secure them from who?" The woman looked down at her feet for a few moments. She knew her answer would not help her case.

"From Those For, sir. Readings taken from The Foundation indicate the presence of anti-matter storage facilities at various installations around Syracuse."

Syracuse.

Everyone in the room sat up straight at the mention of that place. Even Hinds, hiding outside, held his breath as she spoke of it. The city of Syracuse was deep behind enemy lines.

"All we need to do, sir, is get to them."

"That's suicide, Commander. I will not sacrifice my soldiers."

"Respectfully, sir, you already sacrifice them every day."

"Enough!" COL Deeley shouted, returning to his seat. "Even if I were able to get my men past T.F. artillery barrages, anyone who remained would be left to deal with thousands of ground troops and tanks. Syracuse is close on a map but physically a world away. You're asking for a major ground assault, Kelsey. All for something we wouldn't even know what to do with. Where would we even begin if we managed to reach your objective?"

Suddenly, Anirban stood and moved to the center of the floor next to the man and woman in the strange uniforms. "I can take it from there, Colonel. I've spent years researching warp drive technology, and I will vouch for her plan. Get me the anti-matter, and I will build your Drive."

The woman looked more confident now as the colonel's face turned red.

"The fact remains that I will not dedicate my units to a suicidal effort."

"I don't need entire units, sir. Just give me a few soldiers, and we'll find a way."

"You're free to search for volunteers, Commander, but I refuse to put my name to this. I cannot be held responsible for this nonsense that you're planning. I doubt you'll find anyone willing to take that risk."

The room fell silent with his declaration. *Fighting with Delta was supposed to be suicide too,* Hinds thought, realizing there might be a chance, despite the colonel's doubts.

"I'll go," Hinds said, passing through the doors and approaching the panel. "I'll go, and I've got some friends who might want to come too."

VI

I AM WORTHY

Hinds held tightly to his harness as the 5G centrifuge whipped him around the room. It was his third day of spaceflight training, which he had unknowingly agreed to after volunteering with CDR Cochran. Had she mentioned the conditions behind joining her team on The *Foundation* a few days prior, he might not have gone with her. The centrifuge was a large beam attached at its center to an axis around which two carriers on either of its ends revolved at high speeds. It was designed solely to subject aviators to increasing levels of acceleration, just as they would be during flight.

He was losing himself quickly, his body was numb, and he could hardly see. With each second that passed, his vision got worse, narrowing out until everything was black. It was almost as though he had lost consciousness, except he could still feel the crushing pressure against his chest and the dizzying spin of the beam. After what felt like an hour, the machine slowed to a stop, and Hinds stumbled out of his carrier, nearly unable to hold himself upright.

"Fifteen seconds this time." CDR Cochran's voice echoed over the intercom inside the chamber. "I'm disappointed."

Hinds leaned against the beam and looked up at her through a glass dome that encapsulated the centrifuge. She stood with her arms crossed next to Anirban, who was recording notes on his clipboard. They faced each other and mumbled something that was inaudible over the intercom, as they had following his first two tests. His previous rotations in the centrifuge ran for six and ten seconds, respectively, earning him the same disappointment.

"You'll need a full minute in there if we're going to make this work," she continued.

"Make what work?" he asked. "You haven't told me your plan." CDR Cochran and Anirban stared at him briefly and then continued mumbling. "Do you even have a plan?"

"We have one, but you're not going to like it," Anirban finally said. "The only way to get you behind enemy lines without being detected is to drop you in."

"Okay, I'm already trained for that. If it's just a simple airborne jump, then why are we using this?" Hinds pointed to the centrifuge, now motionless but still softly vibrating from its last run.

"You'll be making the jump from orbit, and you won't be using any sort of landing craft. They're too bulky and would be shot from the sky."

"What? So that's it? You're just gonna toss me out into space?"

"You and the friends you so graciously volunteered. We've never attempted orbital freefall, but with the right equipment, it should work. We can use a transport to get you within the mesosphere where you'll make the drop. From there, we'll navigate you as close to Syracuse as we can. Once you touch down, it's on you."

"They'll shoot at us anyway once we get close enough, landing craft or not. They'll see our 'chutes, even in total darkness."

"Then you'll need to deploy them at the very last possible second to avoid detection. It will have to be an extremely high altitude jump with an extremely low parachute opening. There are risks. We might do everything right and still fail, but judging by your record, you should be used to that by now," CDR Cochran said. The pair regarded each other solemnly for a long while, with the understanding that there would be no returning from this one, should even the slightest misfortune occur.

"Now that we've discussed the jump," Anirban said, breaking the unforgiving silence, "I think it's time to figure out the more difficult task of extraction. When—if you manage to secure the anti-matter, what is the plan to get you safely back to friendly lines? It's a dense package. You won't be able to move it very far on foot."

"Depends on whether or not we're detected, I guess," Hinds said, still noticeably overwhelmed by the concept of a jump from orbit. He wasn't sure why they were even planning anything beyond that part of the mission since they'd probably all die in the process anyway. "Do you have a map we could look at?"

The commander moved the group over to an old physical map seated on a large table in the corner of the room just outside the glass dome. It was covered with chess pieces, symbolizing outdated battle positions from a few weeks prior.

"Say these pawns each represented T.F. infantry companies made up of two-hundred Soldiers each, the knights are tank companies, ten tanks strong, and the queen is our objective." Hinds arranged the pieces into a barrier around Syracuse, with pawns scattered all around, tanks at the eastern boundary, and the objective at the city center. "This doesn't account for enemy air defense, aerial TI-84 patrols, or fortifications. Assuming we're not killed by flak during entry, compromised by roving infantry, or rolled on by the tanks, our best bet will be to aim for the city center and retrograde west."

"How do you know these positions are accurate?" Anirban asked.

"I don't. This is just my best guess based on my previous engagements with T.F. The fight is coming from the east, so they would obviously keep their tanks east for defense. As for the anti-matter, I doubt they'd store it anywhere near the fight, but I can't be sure. So we'll have to land in the center and search west. Once we find it, we steal it and push outside city limits for extraction." He placed the king one-hundred kilometers west of the city center. "That will be our rally point."

"And how will you move the anti-matter? A handful of it could way more than one-hundred pounds, and we'll need a lot more than that to build a warp drive."

Hinds thought for a moment.

"We'll find transportation behind the lines. T.F. officers conduct mounted battlefield circulation to check on their guys. Shouldn't be hard to ambush one and take their truck."

"You sound confident about that," CDR Cochran said.

"I figure if we even get to that point, we'll be invincible. Once we push west with the package, the ball is back in your court. How do you plan on getting us out of there?"

"I know a pilot who just might be willing to make that trip. An old colleague of mine who I used to train. She's a lieutenant as well, or perhaps a captain now, I think. If anyone can fly around enemy lines without being seen, it's her. I'll have her meet you at the extraction point."

"If these pieces fall into place as we've said here, we may actually pull this off," Anirban said, satisfied.

"Assuming we don't get compromised," Hinds reminded him sternly. "If we're seen, that changes the game. We'll be surrounded by an infinitely large enemy force in a matter of minutes."

"The newspapers tell me you've dealt with something like that before too." Anirban smiled and folded his arms. "This can be done, young man. Let us dare to see it done, for mankind's sake."

The three of them stared down at the map, an image of what would be the greatest and most difficult military operation in recent history, should any of this crew manage to survive.

***

CDR Cochran flew the emergency transport roughly ten-thousand feet above T.A. occupied space in preparation for the first test jump. Onboard, Hinds waited with two other men from the *Foundation* chosen as his team for the jump. Dr. Jorge Pajares and Dr. Ebon Yizar, the resident experts in propulsion mechanics. Their faces were unfamiliar, equally as anonymous and untrustworthy as any other civilian who hadn't met the trials of combat. They were built for staff work, having spent a majority of their days observing Elnath from the space station, and it was unlikely that either of them understood the realities of war.

He watched them carefully, laying odds as to whether or not either of them would survive the test jump. "Have you done this before?" Dr. Yizar shouted as the pair of scientists turned their attention toward him.

"Once or twice," he lied, with at least fifteen jumps on his record. On the other end of the cabin, the cockpit door opened, and CDR Cochran stepped through.

"Gentlemen, we've nearly arrived." She walked over to a console at the cabin's center and loaded a visual of their objective. "For this test run, we'll be infiltrating some familiar territory—Randall's Island."

Hinds clenched his teeth together. It had been a while since he last reported to his unit. No one had seen him since the fight on the island, and he would likely be AWOL by now. Subject to arrest if they were caught.

"Yes, Lieutenant, you're AWOL," the commander said, reading his thoughts. "There are posters with your face on them. Since this mission isn't sanctioned by the top brass, it can't be used as an excuse for your absence, nor can we bail you out if you're apprehended — much like how the real mission will be."

"Understood, ma'am."

"Your target is the UNIVAC 5000 located inside the island's operations center. You'll jump in, secure it and retrograde across the bridge where my pilot will extract you. Any questions?"

"Just one, ma'am. How do we get past the island's defenses...?" Hinds asked bluntly. The plan seemed incomplete, as though she hadn't accounted for resistance.

"That's up to you to figure out. You should be an expert since this is your duty station. You'll have until sunrise to reach the extraction point, which gives you about eight hours. If you haven't reached it by then, I guess I'll have to find a new team." The commander returned to her seat in the cockpit and left the three to prepare. "Five minutes to drop zone," she said loudly over the intercom.

Hinds quickly rallied his team toward the display. "Check this out," he said. "I'm going to jump first. You two stay close behind me. We're gonna have to land right at the edge of the bridge to avoid being blown out of the sky. No parachutes until about four thousand feet, understood?"

The scientists stared at him with no response. *We're doomed.*

"Once we touch down, we'll have to low-crawl to Delta Company, where we'll wait for shift change. That will be our only opportunity to get in there without being seen. Has anyone worked with a 5000 before? I don't know how to disconnect one."

"I have," Dr. Pajares said. "It's not difficult, but once we remove it, the entire operation's center will shut down."

"That'll probably trigger an installation lockdown, making it much harder to leave the island."

"Two minutes to drop zone."

"We'll have to improvise," Hinds continued. "After we retrieve it, we'll low-crawl back to the bridge and ambush a patrol vehicle. We can use its crew to bypass bridge security."

"Sounds easy enough," Dr. Yizar said. "How do you low-crawl?"

"Oh man. Just follow my lead and do everything I do. Otherwise, we're gonna run into problems. He closed the display, moved over to the cargo hatch, and strapped on his parachute for the jump. "One more thing. The weapons we're carrying with us are just for show. Those are my guys down there. We're not shooting anybody, even if they shoot at us."

"Sixty seconds to drop zone."

All three fell in line next to one another as the hatch opened and revealed ten thousand feet of dark, open space below. They were jumping into oblivion. It would be nearly impossible to navigate under these conditions, but still, they had to try. Everything depended on it.

"Ten seconds to drop zone."

"Get ready!"

"Five…four…three…two…one…"

And they jumped.

***

Twenty seconds of free-fall until they had to open their parachutes, which was as close as Hinds would cut it. If everything worked out, that would leave the team just enough space to glide over the river toward the edge of the bridge— and it would allow time to deploy the reserve chutes if the main ones failed.

Through the intense darkness, all they could see was a faint outline of the island and the obstruction lights that lined the towers at each end of the bridge preventing aircraft collision. So far, there was no alarm, no incoming flak, and no sign that the team was detected, a smooth passage that Hinds was unused to. There was always something that went wrong.

Ten seconds in, he flipped his body and searched the sky behind him for the scientists. He found their traces descending in a staggered formation a few hundred feet above him. They weren't new to this, it seemed, as novice jumpers typically spun out immediately upon exiting a craft and fell through the air like coins being tossed. These two were steady, steadier than he, in fact.

Hinds waved his hands twice, signaling to his team that two-thousand feet were remaining until they had to deploy their parachutes. Both scientists copied the gesture, acknowledging receipt. At twenty seconds, it was time, and each of them pulled their release mechanisms simultaneously, launching a group of canopies into the air above them.

If anyone wanted to see them coming, now was their chance. Their footprint in the sky was impossible to miss, even under the cover of darkness. Still nothing. The team continued to pass by unnoticed as their formation descended over the bridge toward the island. They landed at its edge and touched down beneath a small cliff, which barely concealed them as they packed away and discarded their canopies.

"Two hours until shift change. "Hinds said, checking his watch. "We'll have to move quickly. There's a lot of ground to cover." He clambered up the cliff-face to view the path ahead. There were easily five miles between them and the operations center that would have to be carefully navigated— armed patrols were random here. Two or three-man teams made spot checks on arbitrary sections of the island, courtesy of CPT Sullivan, who was paranoid even before the recent attack. No doubt security had doubled up since then.

"How long will we have during the shift change?" Dr. Yizar asked.

"Not long. Maybe thirty minutes at best, during which time all of the leadership on the island will gather at a terrain model about one hundred meters behind the operations center. There, they'll discuss events that took place during the shift." Hinds jumped down from the wall. "Dr. P, you'll have to go in there alone and get that 5000 out fast. Can you do it?"

"I can try," he replied quietly, his face pale.

"Good. Let's go over this one more time." He grabbed a stick and began to sketch a diagram of the plan in the sand. "We'll move from here to the crater closest to the operations center. Once we arrive, we can rest and wait until shift change. When everyone is outside, Dr. P will run in, snatch the 5000 and meet us back in the crater. Understand?"

The scientists nodded silently.

"Good. Next, we'll move back to the bridge and wait for the first patrol vehicle to pass. Once it is near, I'll run forward and ambush the driver. As soon as I do that—and I mean the very second the vehicle stops—I'll need you both to run forward and ambush any other passengers in the vehicle. We'll steal it and ride across the bridge to extraction. Clear?"

No response.

"We'll adjust as necessary. Just don't get caught. I don't need that sort of trouble in my life right now."

The team climbed over the ridge, maintaining a low profile as they began to crawl forward, inching their way toward the island's center. Movement across the field was rigorous, as the terrain hadn't been reset from the battle weeks before. The group was forced to maneuver in and out of deep craters, a task that was almost impossible from a low-crawl position.

"Wait," Hinds whispered loudly, raising a fist in the air and bringing his party to a halt. Directly in front of them, a disk-shaped mound protruded slightly above the surface. "Land mines." They had no way of detecting them. "Dr. P, you and your friend need to carefully get behind me. Stay a couple feet apart and keep your spacing. Do exactly as I do."

The pair eased slowly behind the lieutenant, each without taking a single breath, fearing that the slightest shift would send them to their maker, a pink mist scattered in the wind. Without even looking back, Hinds began to crawl forward once again, negotiating a path around the mine. They continued in a line-formation for what felt like days until they were within sight of the operations tent.

"What do you see?" Dr. Pajares asked, completely out of breath from the journey. Dr. Yizar had fallen behind and was still struggling to catch up to the others, who had come to a stop on the inside of a shallow crater.

"They're gathered behind the tent. Fifteen or twenty of them. We're a little late." Hinds turned toward the group and leaned against the crater wall. "No time for rest, Doc. Looks like this is it."

Dr. Pajares crawled forward, withdrew a pair of optics from his kit, and observed the gathering behind the tent. A captain, two lieutenants, and a crowd of enlisted soldiers were discussing plans around a map.

"What do I do if there's someone inside?" he asked.

"Just act like you're a member of Delta. Only some low-ranking joe would be in there now, and they won't know the difference nor care anyway."

"Okay, here I go." Dr. Pajares stowed his optics and dashed forward, diving to the ground in three-second intervals to avoid detection. He quickly arrived at the tent's entrance and slipped inside.

"What now?" Dr. Yizar asked.

"Now we wait."

Dr. Pajares was certainly taking his time. Fifteen minutes had passed, and the two remaining in the crater saw no sign of his success. Hinds checked his watch. It was 0430, which gave them a little less than two hours until sunrise. Their retreat would have to be quick.

"Here he comes," Dr. Yizar said. He watched as Jorge bolted out of the tent.

Behind him, the shift-change brief was coming to an end. Delta's staff was going back to work, and Jorge managed to jump back into cover just as CPT Sullivan looked in his direction. The team went prone, planting themselves as close to the ground as possible and waiting.

Minutes later, there was no sign of alarm, at least not yet, but it wouldn't be long before CPT Sullivan realized the 5000 was missing.

"We don't have much time. Let's get moving." The team began to crawl once again, retracing the exact path they took on the way in. The air was tense as they made their advance. Silhouettes circled them in groups of two, often passing within fifty feet of their trail. Patrols scanning the open space between the tent and the bridge were appearing more frequently—they were looking for them now.

Hinds took a risk and diverted the team away from their initial path into a nearby trench, the same one his platoon had dug for cover during their last fight.

"We need to wait here a minute. Dr. P, do you need me to carry your pack?" Jorge let his bag fall from his shoulders, and it hit the ground with a thud. The UNIVAC 5000 was not a small piece of equipment. It added almost one hundred pounds to his already heavy kit. "No, I've got it. Why did we stop here?"

"I think I heard a vehicle off in the distance. It might be making rounds to check on security." Hinds leaned over the trench with his optics and saw a patrol car driving toward Kennedy. Inside, he spotted a driver and one passenger. Shifting his field of view back to the bridge, he found a single soldier standing guard on the road.

"Is that it?"

"Yeah, there's a guard on the bridge. It's going to check on him. We're gonna have to take this one. We don't have time to wait for another pass."

He glanced at his watch. Thirty minutes to extraction. The team was still a fair distance away from the bridge, and there was no way to determine how much time they would have to make the drop on the vehicle.

"Gents, I'm gonna try and beat it to the bridge, detain the guard and ambush the car once it arrives. As soon as they pull up, you need to run forward and secure them from behind. You'll need to run faster than you ever have in your life because I'll be outnumbered three-to-one if you don't get there on time."

Without waiting for a reply, Hinds jumped over the trench wall and dashed forward toward the bridge—a familiar play. He closed the distance in seconds and found the guard leaning against a wall, asleep at his post. Quickly, he placed him in a chokehold and held an empty sidearm to his head. The guard didn't make a sound, nor did he seem to recognize his captor. Hinds read the nameplate inscribed on the back of his helmet. It was SGT Radd, a soldier assigned to the Military Police Platoon. He had seen him in the trenches shortly before T.F. attacked the island.

"Don't move a muscle when that truck pulls up," he ordered. The vehicle stopped directly in front of them with bright lights that completely obscured its occupants. Up above, hanging from a comms antenna, was an officer's flag bearing the captain rank insignia.

"Put the weapon down, Hinds. Whatever this is, it's over." It was Lehman. Hinds did nothing and waited for his team to make a move. "I will shoot you. Release my soldier and drop your weapon." Still, he did nothing as the beads of sweat slid down his face and betrayed his confidence. He wondered whether the scientists had been caught or if they simply froze up. Then he heard a metal click and prepared for the blast.

"Stop right there." They had arrived, creeping up behind the vehicle with empty weapons in hand. Caught off guard, Lehman and her driver surrendered their arms to the scientists.

"Keep them in the car," Hinds ordered. "They're coming with us."

The team shoved the patrol members and the guard into the back of the car and continued to hold them at gunpoint. "I'll drive." He jumped in the front seat and sped down the bridge, with only ten minutes remaining until extraction.

"What the hell is going on here?" Lehman asked. "Where have you been?" She was furious. If she lashed out now and called their bluff, they would be in serious trouble.

"I need your help. With something more important than the war."

"Are you kidding me? There's a warrant out for your arrest. I can't be seen with you. All that hero nonsense went out the window when you decided not to report back to base."

"LT," Dr. Pajares interrupted. "That's the bird up above." It was a standard rotary-wing chopper—old but tougher to detect at night than modern aircraft. Hinds slammed the breaks as they reached the extraction point, hard enough to knock his team over and allow the detainees to reach their weapons. Lehman was out of the car first, aimed at the rest of the group. Her driver and the guard quickly followed suit, covering the vehicle's flanks.

"None of you are going anywhere. Get on the ground and put your hands behind your backs."

"Lehman, you're making a mista—"

"Now," she demanded. The team reluctantly fell from the sides of the truck. Ahead of them, the chopper landed, and its pilot ran toward the scene with her sidearm at the ready.

"Paige!" she shouted, struggling to project her voice over the roaring aircraft. Lehman finished tying Hinds 'arms behind his back and turned to find CPT Cortese running toward her.

"Ryan? What are you doing here?"

"She's our ri—" Lehman kicked Hinds in the stomach firmly, silencing him. CPT Cortese knelt beside the team and inspected the identification tags around their necks.

"Dr. Pajares, I'm Captain Ryan Cortese. I was sent here to get you by Commander Cochran."

VII

RAIN

"This ride is tougher than I remember," Dr. Yizar said as he bounced in his seat.

The crew was en route to the Terminal via subway to begin training as a complete team—with the members they had recruited against their will. CDR Cochran spun them up on the mission status thus far while Anirban sat with Hinds and the other scientists recovering from their test at the other end of the car. The lieutenant was unusually quiet as he watched Paige and Ryan next to each other, bracing against one another when the train passed over debris. He was unsettled by the thought that he was too late.

"How long has it been since you've been down here?" Dr. Pajares replied.

"A few years. Not since it was built, I think. I haven't even been back on 189 for a while."

"You should come down from the Foundation more often. Extended spaceflight isn't good for your bones." Just then, the train shifted violently, nearly throwing Dr. Yizar and Anirban out of their seats.

"But this is?"

Anirban stood and held onto the overhead support, placing himself in between the groups at each end of the car.

"Gentlemen, I want to share the current operation concept that the commander and I have developed. You're all aware that the purpose of your orbital insertion is to retrieve anti-matter, correct?" All but Hinds nodded. "That resource will be used in the construction of a warp drive, which we intend to use for interstellar travel." He paused in anticipation of some argument from the other three and found none. The scientists were already aware of the idea, for the most part.

"So there are no other options then?" Dr. Yizar asked. "We absolutely have to leave the system?"

"Precisely. We've war-gamed every other plan, and all of them end in destruction. We have come to the point where we must either leave or die."

"I assume we won't be able to move more than a few hundred people with the ships Those Against has."

"Kelsey and I are headed to meet with the T.A. Commander to ask for his help. We intend to put a larger fleet together, somehow. For now, focus on the jump. We'll take care of the rest." The group was silent. The introduction of such an incomplete plan made them question the risk they were taking with the orbital drop. The pair had yet to convince COL Deeley of anything.

Anirban looked down at Hinds, who was still entirely focused on the captains on the other end of the car. "Are you okay young man?"

"He's probably still recovering from that kick to the stomach!" Dr. Pajares laughed.

"Tell me, are you close with the captain you brought along?"

"I don't know," he replied, for the first time this entire trip. The others watched him with half-smiles on their faces, having come to a shared conclusion about his current state.

"Why would you volunteer someone you love for this mission?" Dr. Pajares asked.

"She's my closest friend. The only person I knew for sure would come with me." He turned to look at her once again, and at the same moment, she broke eye contact with the commander and gave him her usual cold and unforgiving stare.

She just found out what I've really gotten her into. He quickly looked away and faced the ground.

"Have you told her yet?" Anirban asked.

Hinds said nothing, and the group continued to watch the lieutenant in silence for the remainder of the journey.

"You're running out of opportunities, young man. We may not have much time. None of us."

***

"A planet-wide evacuation?" COL Deeley grew noticeably frustrated as he struggled to tolerate the newest revision to CDR Cochran's plan. "Kelsey, that's a little above my pay-grade."

Once again, she stood with Dr. Acharya on the floor of COL Deeley's panel, petitioning for his support. This time, however, he sat alone without his staff and the banter they typically brought with them. "Say I could order this. What is your plan to rescue the billions of people on 189?"

"Sir, with enough manpower, we could have a fleet of ships assembled inside the Terminal within a year." She fought to keep from clenching her fists in anticipation of his disapproval.

"And where will you go? Have you actually managed to build a warp drive?"

"I'm nearly complete with the schematics, sir." Anirban stepped forward to the 5000 and panned the projection at the center of the room out beyond their current star system to a scale that the machine could not process in real-time. He froze it just above the southwestern quadrant of the galaxy and drew a line from Corina-189 to the nearest neighboring stars, continuing in a straight path to the galactic edge. "Colonel, I'll be able to construct a drive that will move us at speeds just under that of light. Given that capability, or constraint, if you will, we can go as far as the edge of the galaxy in our lifetime. I've highlighted the best potential star systems for your review."

COL Deeley approached the projection and hovered over the highlighted stars. None of them were particularly close, and none of them were close to one another. From their current distance, the projection wasn't able to display planets harbored by each of these stars nor atmospheric data related to habitability. It wouldn't be able to provide any real certainty until they flew within range of each system.

Disappointed, he returned to his seat and focused the 5000 back onto Elnath. The sliver of natural light protruding from the sphere was even smaller now, which made finding it on the projection noticeably more difficult. That alone was persuasive enough to convince him. He sighed deeply and began drafting notes on a sheet of paper.

"Kelsey, typically, I would never stand behind a plan that was only forty percent complete, but time is not on our side.

Three-thousand Soldiers, all of those who aren't directly engaged in the fight with the enemy. That is what I can give you. The rest must remain on the front lines to keep us from being overrun."

"Thank you, sir." her voice trembled at his response — she had never expected him to agree, not in this lifetime, not for a million years.

"No need. They will be stationed at Randall's within the next few days once we decide where to take them from. Fortune favors the brave and the bold, Kelsey. Don't let us down."

***

"They might just reach the one-minute mark," Anirban said. He watched alongside the team leaders as SGT Radd and SGT Root completed another centrifuge test. "But none of that matters if you compromise yourselves during the mission." He was referring to their last training jump a few days prior, where they were tasked with evading the Terminal's aerial sensors. The six of them had exited the aircraft at forty-thousand feet with the intention of deploying their parachutes at four-thousand, but Lehman pulled hers too early and gave away the team's position.

She was particularly bitter ever since then, refusing to engage in any conversation that didn't require important information from her. The anger she felt toward Hinds was clear and unmistakable. He had destroyed her career by forcing her to abandon her post at Randall's as he did. The two hadn't spoken since her capture.

"At the very least, you are making progress," Anirban continued. "The commander wants an evacuation fleet built by the year's end."

"A fleet? Where?"

"Right here at the Terminal. A fleet of carriers."

"So I guess we're not taking everybody, then." Hinds remembered seeing a carrier once, not long before the war, when the sphere components were brought up to Elnath. It was like a massive cruise ship in the sky—but even a fleet of them couldn't save everyone on 189.

"No, but we'll take as many as we can." The centrifuge slowed to a halt, and both Sergeants remained conscious as it crawled past the one-minute mark. "They've done it. That makes four of you." He turned and stared at the two officers, waiting for an explanation as to why they hadn't met the standard.

"Paige, wanna go for a run?" Hinds asked. As he expected, she didn't respond, nor did she seem to acknowledge that he was speaking to her. Disappointed, he left for the centrifuge on his own.

Anirban continued to watch Lehman as she stood silent. "You're not exempt from training, Captain."

"I don't care, old man. I shouldn't even be here."

"But you are here. Hinds may have brought you to us, but he isn't forcing you to stay." Indeed he wasn't. It was Ryan. Once Lehman realized Ryan was a part of this, there was no way she could leave. Still, she couldn't admit that— love wasn't her style. She needed someone to blame, and Hinds was the obvious target. She nearly fell deep into the memory of her flight with Ryan and their first kiss but was distracted by the screeching start of the centrifuge as it began to rotate.

"And if you intend to stay," Anirban went on, "You may as well try as he tries, especially since he's only doing this for you."

"What?" The centrifuge slowed to a halt, interrupting them again. Hinds burst out of the cockpit with his hands raised in the air.

"One minute!" he shouted. He had finally achieved the minimum standard required for the orbital drop. Hinds jumped down from the machine and fell flat on the ground as his feet made contact. He had fainted.

"He'll need some more work, still," Anirban said. "Sergeants, please give me a hand with him." The three of them ran over, loaded him onto a stretcher, and brought him to the medical bay.

Lehman waited, watching the centrifuge as it hummed quietly against the silent backdrop of the room. Once her friend was carried away and all the others had left, she slowly approached the machine and entered.

***

Kelsey Cochran released her safety harness and stood as her transport shuttle prepared to dock at the Terminal. A week had passed since she presented her plan to COL Deeley, during which they had scouted T.A. installations across 189 building manpower for the operation. He was receptive to her ideas, it seemed. As long as he remained so, the numbers they gathered could have a fleet prepared for departure inside of six months.

The commander disembarked the ship and hurried along her usual path to the centrifuge chamber. Inside, she found Anirban working nervously on the schematics for the faster-than-light warp drive that would carry the fleet.

"Where's the crew?" she asked.

"I've sent them to New Rochelle for some R&R a few days ago. It's well deserved. They've all progressed significantly during training."

"Are they ready for the jump?"

"They'd better be. We don't have any time left for more training."

Cochran seated herself at her desk nearby, and both sat silent for a long while.

"I'm starting to think that the jump will be the easiest part of this whole operation."

"Having doubts?" Anirban asked.

"No." Her face told a different story as her lips sank into a frown at their odds of success. "Think about it, though. We're building this huge fleet, and we're just gonna get it into space undetected? Really? T.F. will blow them out of the sky immediately."

Anirban continued his draft, oblivious to her remarks. "One step at a time, Commander. Solve problems as they arrive, don't create them. You're not allowed to be pessimistic as the leader."

"You're not even a little bit worried?"

"I think that whatever is meant to happen will happen. Besides, by the time we're ready to launch, I doubt this war will matter to anyone anymore."

"I wish I shared the same resolve, sir." She stood next to him and watched over his shoulder as he worked. The draft was complex, far beyond her level of scientific understanding, but he built it as though the concept was basic. "How is it coming along?"

"Well, this is all just theory. A composition that has never been orchestrated—but the numbers add up. We can create it, a sort of warp drive that will engulf the fleet in a bubble, compress the space in its path and expand that space behind it, propelling us forward." He looked up at her and read the skepticism in her eyes once again. "Mankind has done crazier things, Kelsey. There was a time when they strapped a man to a rocket and lit the fuse, sending him to space alone, and it worked. Try to have faith."

"How fast can it go?"

"Just under the speed of light, which is all we'll need to reach star systems that may potentially support life. There are a few downsides, though."

"What's wrong?"

"Well, for starters, we'll only have enough fuel to start and stop the drive once. Even with all the fuel available to T.A, we won't be able to maneuver or adjust in-flight."

"So one chance to get the trajectory right."

"Exactly. We still need to determine the path that will expose us to the greatest number of stars, but I'll work on that issue when the kids return with the anti-matter…Anything else bothering you, Commander?"

She faced away from him now, ashamed of her own doubt. "I've been thinking about the evacuation plan."

"What about it?"

"I have none. How do I decide who lives and who dies?"

"Most will choose to stay behind since they don't believe the sphere poses a threat. As for the others—"

"First-come, first-served?"

"Precisely. Members of T.A. closest to the Terminal and most deserving of escape, since they believed from the beginning."

Again, both went silent, with the sound of Anirban's pen echoing across the hangar and through eternity, it seemed.

***

"Aye, yer friends're a strange pair."

McGregor pulled out a glass for Hinds as he watched the two scientists dancing clumsily with some local women to the tune of Lawrence Welk's "The Moon is a Silver Dollar."

"What'll it be?"

"Something strong."

"You hurtin' boy?" He drew a jar of his own personally brewed moonshine from the bottom shelf and filled the glass. Hinds was hurting. Somehow, he knew that one way or another, this would be his final trip home.

"McGregor, you need to get out of here. Leave for the Terminal as soon as you can." The bartender's lips fell into a frown momentarily but quickly resumed their usual aggressive smile.

"Not a chance, boy. I've heard about yer plan. People talk."

"So why are you still here?"

"Captain stays with 'is ship."

Hinds knew he would say that.

"The ship is sinking…189 is done for."

"So be it. She's done a lotta good for me…given me everything. I won't be leavin'er behind, lad."

The lieutenant was silent for a while, oblivious even to the loud music in the background. Then he stood and shook the bartender's hand. "Thanks for everything."

"Aye. Save as many as ye can."

They both sat down across from each other and shared one last drink. Just as they finished, the two scientists came stumbling over to the bar, crashing into the stools right next to Hinds, still filled with excitement from the dance.

"LT, you're missing the party!" Jorge shouted. Frank Sinatra's "One for My Baby" was playing loudly over the jukebox speakers now. As it began, the crowd behind them erupted in a cheer.

"I think I'll sit this one out, guys."

"He's too heavy to dance with all that gold in his pocket anyway!" Ebon shouted. "Have you shown him the ring?"

"Ring? Ye holdin 'out on me, boy?" The three of them watched in anticipation as he slowly pulled out a small black box. Inside was a gold wedding ring he had bought that afternoon. It was for Lehman, should either of them survive the jump.

"Jesus…how much did 'ye spend on it, boy?" McGregor nearly dropped his glass when he saw it.

"Every last dollar I had."

"He's not kidding. He actually has no money left. These drinks are on us," Jorge said.

"Aye…these are on the house. Who's it for? That same lass? Don't tell me—"

"After the mission, yeah."

"We talked about this, boy. Ye need to quit waitin'!!"

"She's not too happy with him right now anyway!" Ebon laughed.

"And they've only recently met!" Jorge chimed in.

Hinds tucked the ring away in his cargo pocket. There was no "right time" to present it. No matter when he did, his dreams of living peacefully and starting a family could never be real. Even if she said yes, those dreams weren't compatible with this version of reality, and that was clear. No one could plan. Still, he knew that he loved her, despite everything. He was sure that before it was all over, he would at least try.

"Aye, pipe down wi'the negativity, lads. Follow yer heart, boy. It'll know what to do."

"No matter what happens, things can't possibly turn out worse than my last marriage." The four of them laughed.

"One more song, then we've gotta go. The next train is the last one back to the Terminal for two days," Jorge said. He ran with Ebon back to their group on the dance floor as the jukebox changed its tune once again to Vera Lynn's "The White Cliffs of Dover."

Hinds stared at his empty glass and listened, thinking of this small town, of his family and friends who he'd likely never see again. He thought of 189, of all his Soldiers who fought and died here, and wondered if he should remain here on the ship too.

There'll be bluebirds over The White Cliffs of Dover tomorrow. Just you wait and see. There'll be love and laughter and peace ever after tomorrow, when the world is free.

✳✳✳

"We've identified two locations west of the city-center likely storage areas for anti-matter." The group sat inside the Terminal's command suite and received a mission brief from CDR Cochran. Today was the day. They had been split into two teams: Lehman, Dr. Yizar, and Dr. Pajares would assault the first target closest to the western boundary, while Hinds, SGT Radd, and SGT Root took the other. "CPT Lehman, LT Hinds, your teams will land east of your targets and search westward through the city center." She panned the 5000's visuals out to an aerial view of Syracuse.

"Patrols will be heavy," Anirban said, stepping forward. "We've spotted at least fifty soldiers moving in groups throughout the city. TI-83s will likely also be present."

The teams stared back at them with blank faces. Despite all of their training, they had very little hope.

"You can do this, guys," Cochran said in a weak effort to reassure them. She knew, however, that if they didn't try and succeed, all of them were dead anyway.

"We know, boss. Don't worry about us," Jorge replied.

"Will we have any support?" Lehman asked.

"Yes." COL Deeley, who had been watching the brief from the back of the room, stood and addressed them. "The soldiers remaining on the front lines east of Syracuse will mount a concentrated assault on the city. At the very least, that should distract their mounted and armored units. They'll remain engaged until we get word that you've been safely extracted. Make haste—our numbers won't last long against reinforced T.F. units."

They all remained silent for a long time. For a while, it seemed everything was quiet. Even the usual clamor of personnel transferring in and out of the trains above faded away. COL Deeley didn't say it outright, but the somber tone of his voice made it clear that those soldiers would be making their last stand. He looked down at his watch and began packing his notes into his briefcase. "Kelsey, is there anything else you need from me?"

"No, sir, you've given us more than we could ask for."

"I'll be standing by for updates. My troops will move as soon as your team makes the jump."

"Understood, sir." CDR Cochran called the room to attention, and all parties rendered him a customary salute. As he reached the door, COL Deeley stopped to address them.

"Many soldiers have died fighting this war, and there are more deaths to come still. Secure victory and make their sacrifices count." Then he turned and left, his personal guard falling in beside him as they disappeared into the endless maze of the Warren.

"We take off in one hour," Cochran said. " Use that time to settle any unfinished business you have before we go."

The team returned to their temporary quarters in the Terminal, all except for CPT Lehman, who stayed behind with Anirban and the commander, who remained silent as she approached them. She hesitated—just by looking at them, she could feel the shared weight of their responsibility. They were calm, but their eyes were tired. It had likely been some time since they had taken a break or slept.

"Ma'am, I just wanted to ask what you felt about our odds of success," she said finally.

Cochran smiled softly. "I feel that the odds don't matter. Stay oblivious to the impossible, and you'll get it done, just like any other mission."

"Understood."

"Clear your mind, Captain. It may be a long while before we have another moment of peace. Once we take off, it's game on."

Lehman left for her quarters, hoping the commander believed her own words.

***

Employees shuffled past Lehman as she hurried back to her quarters. Behind them were the soldiers brought in from the front lines to assemble the fleet. The group was headed to the Terminal's launch area, where space was currently being cleared out to make room for the fifteen ships that would carry them away from 189. Fifteen ships: Five civilian carriers, five cargo ships, and five reserves carrying emergency water, food, and fuel.

Lehman couldn't shake the thought of the thousands of people who would risk everything to reach the Terminal, only to discover once they arrived that there was either no room or not enough room to take their families. This was a major problem that no one discussed, despite its inevitability. She figured the brass had already determined a solution—perhaps they planned on using the soldiers now stationed here to repel the crowds once the manifest was complete.

Hopefully, they're better than that, she thought.

The door to her section opened up to a small room with two cots stacked in bunks on each side, though she only shared this room with Ryan. Alone, she sat at her bunk and pulled a photo from beneath her pillow. The pair had taken it together, smiling beneath a statue in New Rochelle on their first day of R&R. It was the only time she could remember being truly happy.

Lehman tucked the photo inside her pocket and prepared to return to the launchpad for departure. As she stood, she noticed a small black box sitting atop an end table in the corner of the room. In front of it was an envelope with a note inside.

I'll never abandon you, Lehman. No matter the circumstances or the odds against us.

– Hinds

Lehman held her breath, opened the box, and found a gold wedding ring. She was immediately frozen with anger at Hinds for entering her quarters and leaving this in the open for Ryan to find. Yet, at the same time, she found herself fighting away tears. He was her best friend, though she would never say it, and she had always treated him poorly.

Still, he cared for her despite everything. She placed the ring on a chain around her neck, beside her identification tags. Deep down, Lehman knew she never wanted to lose him either, but she couldn't marry him—her heart belonged to Ryan.

"There you are." Lehman quickly wiped her face and turned to find Ryan standing at the door. "You okay?"

"Yeah, just a little nervous, is all."

"You're the strongest woman I know, and you have a good team. I know you'll be fine." She leaned over and kissed her. "I have something to ask you before you go."

***

She arrived with Ryan twenty minutes late, reaching the launchpad as the team was nearly finished donning their equipment: Bulky suits built to withstand the varying pressures of the jump. She began to put hers on, desperately avoiding eye contact with the others as they waited for her by the transport. Looking up briefly, Lehman saw Hinds staring at her engagement ring—the one Ryan gave her at their quarters. He was in a trance, struggling to remain upright. She had broken his heart and his mind right before the mission. She couldn't bear to face him.

Those who knew quietly observed his pain before CDR Cochran directed them to board the transport, marching them in line to the craft. Hinds was the last to enter, waiting from afar as Ryan buttoned up the sides of the suit that Lehman couldn't reach.

"Be safe, sweetheart," Ryan said, placing herself between the two. Hinds turned away slowly and joined the others. Lehman only nodded as she retrieved her helmet and followed him.

The team gave CDR Cochran a thumbs-up once they were strapped into their seats with their helmets on, and within seconds, they were off. The ship quickly flipped into a vertical position and ascended through the Terminal's outer shield into 189's open sky.

"Systems green," she said. It was nearly impossible to hear the commander over the comms.

The transport climbed rapidly, growing more unsteady with each passing minute. Lehman turned to her right and watched through the window as 189's surface receded beneath her until there was nothing but clouds below and a darkening sky above. She examined the crew, each of them holding fast to the harness that kept them in place. Opposite her was her friend, cold and indifferent in his suit, seemingly unaware of the violent tremors around him.

"One-hundred thousand feet," CDR Cochran continued. "Standby." The ship began to settle as it broke through the outer layers of the atmosphere. Moments later, the ship slowed to a halt and pivoted to face the planet.

Then, there it was before them. Corina-189, shining brilliantly under the dwindling cover of Elnath. It was the first time most of them had ever seen it. The orb was a cloudy blue, dotted with frequent but tiny bursts of light that appeared on its surface. All of the conflict they had ever known, every battle that had ever been fought in human history, took place down there.

And still, it was beautiful.

"Team," the commander said, pulling Lehman from her brief respite. "Initiate jump in ten…nine…"

She forced her eyes away from the planet and turned again toward Hinds, who was already staring at her.

"Five…four…three…"

Time seemed to freeze, slowing the seconds into hours as they looked at one another. Neither was able to see a face through the dark helmet lenses, but somehow they could read one another's thoughts: Here they were once more, jumping into the unknown together.

"Be safe," he finally said softly. *I love you.*

"Watch your back out there." *I love you too.*

Then the hatch opened, and the escaping oxygen rushed away with the words unsaid. The teams split in mid-air, separating the two before they even realized their last chance was gone.

They tumbled frantically toward the planet, fighting to stabilize themselves against their incredible spin. Beneath her, Lehman could see the cloud deck quickly approaching, and she grabbed ahold of her team to avoid losing sight of them.

The three of them fell through the dense cloud cover in a stable formation, emerging on the other side to intense gunfire—cannons on the surface firing in their direction, either at them or at some unknown aircraft near their position. The incoming flak was so thick, Lehman thought she could step forward and walk across it.

She searched for the other team and found them just before a burst of shrapnel exploded near the group. With a quick flash, two of them were gone, blasted away into the surrounding abyss. Lehman's mind went blank, and her vision narrowed—she felt her consciousness slipping away.

At this point, she had lost her team's position relative to the ground and was no longer sure when to deploy her parachute. Just before she completely faded away, a hand reached through the darkness and grabbed hers, bringing her close enough to pull the cord at her waist. Then it was gone, and she descended through the void alone.

VIII

HOPE

CPT Lehman awoke on the floor of an abandoned house that had been severely damaged by T.A. aircraft. She lay watching the sky through the shattered lens of her helmet as the ships circled quickly above, dodging the perpetual bursts of flak. T.F. had been aiming at those ships. It was COL Deeley's supporting assault force. Lehman sat up, discarded her headgear, and scrambled over to the scientists who were guarding the exposed area of a destroyed wall.

"Where are we?" she asked, kneeling next to Jorge and aiming through the scope of her weapon.

"Just north of the city's center," Jorge replied. He pulled out his radio and attempted to establish comms with the other team but found nothing but static on the other end.

"How long have comms been down?"

"We never had them. Haven't heard from the others since we jumped."

"Did you see them pull their 'chutes?"

"No…I lost sight of them when I went to pull yours. We almost lost you up there." Jorge packed away his radio and resumed his position on the wall. Lehman fell back, pulled the chain from her neck, and held it in front of her. The ring was scuffed from the landing. Its golden frame scarred down its center. She remembered seeing the other team blown away by flak and was shaken with nausea so overwhelming that she nearly threw up.

"We can't stay here," she said, fighting to steady herself. Ahead of them, they saw a sizable force of armored vehicles and TI-83s moving toward the city's eastern boundary. There were hundreds of them, likely the area's entire defense responding to the colonel's advance.

"Dear God," Jorge whispered.

Lehman climbed the stairs to a terrace on the second floor and observed the enemy through her scope. The colonel's supporting element was doomed. The number remaining on the front wasn't enough to counter this—but they knew that from the start. She cleared her head and focused her sights west.

With a group this large supporting the defense, the city would be mostly empty, save for whatever security elements that stayed behind. She scanned the perimeter and found two fortified positions atop the buildings roughly three-hundred meters away but was unable to see any enemy personnel on guard. She climbed back down, rallied everyone to the doorway opposite the exposed wall, and pointed out the positions to her team.

"Two bunkers, eight o'clock high."

"Are we taking them?" Ebon asked.

"No. Too risky. Follow me. We'll pass through the city indoors as best we can and hug the walls outside when we can't." And so they did, slipping easily past both bunkers and through each building until they reached the city center. They found no signs of an anti-matter storage facility along the way, neither did they encounter any resistance. The team paused and set up security underneath the awning of a department store, searching the area for their objective.

"Where are the civilians?" Jorge asked, noting the unusual absence of what seemed to be the entire population of Syracuse. Lehman continued to stare down her scope without a response. The buildings were dark, the stores were locked up, and there were no vehicles on the roads. She figured whoever was here had enough advanced warning that they were able to flee.

What concerned her right now was the total lack of communication from the other team. They all knew the mission's radio frequency, and even if their radios were damaged during insertion, they could have found another and dialed out. Had they survived, they would surely have made some form of contact by now.

"Do you hear that?" Ebon asked, snatching her away from her thoughts.

It was gunfire. Short bursts from a weapon and the explosion of a single grenade. Then it was quiet. The team quickly ran toward the commotion and found an unmanned TI-83 stationed at the entrance of a small facility, its two guards killed.

"It's good to see you, Captain."

Lehman turned to find SGT Root leaning against a wall, holding her leg in pain. "It's shattered...took some flak during the jump. I'm sorry, ma'am, I can't help you," she said.

"Where are the others?" Lehman moved to bandage what she could of Root's leg.

"There was a burst, and I lost sight of them. By the time I pulled my 'chute, we were separated. I landed alone, crawled here thinking I'd find some shelter but found guards instead."

"Captain, this might be it," Jorge interrupted. All of them looked back at the facility. It was the only one they had seen heavily guarded. "It's exactly where the commander said it would be."

Lehman slung her weapon over her shoulder and reset her radio. "Keep watch here. I'm going inside."

"Alone?" Ebon asked. Without a response, she climbed over the TI-83 and jumped down to the building's entrance. She followed the only available path down a poorly lit hallway toward what resembled a laboratory. It was unremarkable, an empty room with no personnel or guards in sight. All that remained were piles of disorganized paper and a few damaged generators. It looked as though whoever was here had only recently left and took whatever they had with them.

"Ma'am, have you found anything?" Ebon asked a few minutes later over the comms.

"Nothing yet. It's clear. How are we looking on time?"

"Our extraction should be arriving shortly. We've got about three hours to complete our movement. We need to leave soon."

"Secure one of the patrol cars outside and get SGT Root loaded up." Lehman tore through every drawer and file she saw, hoping to find anything at all that would justify this mission, but found nothing.

This is pointless, she thought, briefly leaning against a desk. Then, just as she turned to leave, she caught sight of a map near the entrance displaying the locations of all T.F. facilities in the city.

"Moving to your location now," she told her team, carefully folding the map into her kit. She arrived outside and found Jorge atop the TI-83 watching the east through his optics.

"I can see light infantry returning to the city. The fighting must be over."

"Come look at this," she replied, ignoring his observation and unfolding the map. Jorge signaled for Ebon to start the patrol car and jumped down from the TI-83. "We're standing at an anti-matter refining plant, but there was nothing inside."

"Maybe they moved the completed product elsewhere." Jorge searched the map with his finger. "Maybe here?" It was one of many buildings labeled "storage facility" located along what would have been the other team's route. "Maybe they've found it."

"Assuming they've survived." Again, the brief memory of her friend being struck by flak disturbed her thoughts. She knew that was an unrealistic assumption.

"SGT Root did. So there's a chance," Jorge said as he began his climb back over the TI-83. "We need to go. If those troops reach us, we're done."

Lehman folded her map and looked back at the refining plant. *Once again, it's all on you.*

***

"Sir, are you sure this is what we came for?" SGT Radd waited with LT Hinds thirty minutes later in the shadows behind a warehouse they had just cleared. They had found it—or at least thought they had found it. A single crate filled with a dense, glowing silver material. It was marked with an inscription of early Dyson Sphere schematics and had taken a significant effort to carry it outside.

"This has to be it. It's as heavy as the old man said it would be."

SGT Radd glanced down at the crate with doubt strewn across his face. The commander and the old man had given them no real specifications on what the cargo would look like or how much of it they would need to carry back. They were banking heavily on fortune.

"You think the other team found anything?" he asked.

"I just hope they're okay. If they got hurt, that's on me." Hinds crawled forward a few meters and remained prone, facing up the road in search of approaching vehicles. In the distance, he could see that the fighting between T.F. and COL Deeley's assaulting force had slowed, and the thundering volleys of flak and field artillery had ceased completely. He listened closely for the sound of small-arms fire but heard none.

With the overwhelming numbers they saw leaving the city, it was unlikely that any T.A. targets remained. Hinds rested his head briefly on his rifle and wondered if Delta Company was involved and if they had made it out. It was a suicide mission, after all. The kind they were built for. As he nearly fell asleep, SGT Radd crawled to his position and alerted him to the lights moving toward them.

"Vehicles?" Hinds asked. The lights were faint, each moving individually, so they couldn't be.

"Dismounts. We need to get off the road."

Both of them quickly picked up and bounded back toward the crate.

The team of six infantrymen and an officer seated in a patrol car neared steadily toward them and stopped at the entrance of the warehouse, realizing the entrance had been left open. The officer exited the vehicle and beckoned the others to follow her toward the warehouse, out of earshot of the pair hiding in the shadows.

"Radd," Hinds whispered. "I'll run past them to get their attention. As soon as I do—"

"Take them out. I've got it, sir."

Hinds dashed forward out of concealment and sprinted across the road behind a tree on the other side. The T.F. soldier at the rear noticed him just as he found cover and alerted the patrol commander, who directed three of them forward to investigate. Radd waited until they were within range of the patrol car's mini-gun, then ran to mount it, immediately drawing fire from the officer and her remaining soldiers as he loaded the weapon. Hinds dropped prone as the mini-gun opened up on the soldiers in front of him, killing all three before Radd slumped forward over the weapon and the firing stopped. He had been badly wounded.

Hinds ran up to the vehicle and returned fire with his rifle, killing one of the remaining soldiers as the last two ran inside the warehouse.

"Sir, we need to get out of here." Radd struggled to prop himself back up on the gun, blood dripping profusely from a wound in his stomach. "I can't help you load the cargo."

"That's okay, just rest." Hinds removed his uniform jacket and wrapped it around the wound as best he could, but the bleeding continued. As he drove the patrol car back toward the shadows, alarms around the warehouse perimeter sounded, and vehicles in the distance quickly began approaching their position. Radd fell quietly to the floor of the car, submerged in the ocean of red at his feet, and said nothing more.

***

"We're out of time, Paige. I don't know how much longer we can afford to wait." Ryan jumped down from her cockpit and helped Lehman carry SGT Root onto the aircraft. "Enemy comms say their forces are moving west, so that's it. If the others aren't out by now, they'll never make it out."

Lehman continued scanning the road for any sign of the other team. "He wouldn't give up." Her team arrived at the extraction site atop a hill west of Syracuse thirty minutes ago, and they had already blown their timeline for escape. Looking back toward the city, she found towers with lights flashing red as though alarms had been sounded. "Ryan!" She ran back toward the pilot, who was busy starting up the aircraft for departure. "T.F. is looking for them! They're still out there!"

Her response was too quiet to be heard over the aircraft propellers, but the movement of her lips was clear:

Paige, there's no time.

Lehman ignored her, grabbed her rifle from the cockpit, and took a prone position on the ridge facing Syracuse. She watched the road for what felt like hours, knowing that if an alarm had been sounded, the other team was alive and trying to escape.

A few hundred meters away, a plume of smoke from an explosion disrupted her focus. She shifted her sights to its location and found two patrol cars moving at a high speed toward them.

"Jorge, get over here!" she yelled. Dr. Pajares ran to her side and assumed the same position. "Trace the road from that smoke and tell me what you see." He searched for a moment through his optics and identified the same two vehicles.

"It's them!" he said. "They're being followed!"

"Why isn't he using the mini-gun?" Jorge zoomed in and saw Hinds shooting his pistol from the driver's seat at the vehicle behind him.

"Ma'am, there's no one on the mini-gun!"

Lehman stood with her rifle at the high ready. "Spot the rear driver for me. Let me know when they're within three hundred meters!"

"Five hundred...four hundred..." A bead of sweat slid down the side of her face as the vehicles crept into view. "Three hundred!"

She saw them clearly now. The enemy vehicle had only a single occupant: The driver. Lehman took a deep breath, held it to focus her aim, and fired the impossible shot. Her perception of time slowed as the round tore through the air and connected with the driver's head, nearly lifting her out of the patrol car. Lehman exhaled, and time resumed its normal pace. She watched, almost in a trance, as Hinds drove the patrol car up the hill, nearly crashing into the aircraft.

"I need help!" he shouted, dragging his wounded companion from the vehicle. SGT Radd was covered in blood and, by this point, unresponsive. He was hardly breathing. All rushed to his aid save for CPT Cortese, who had only left her seat to secure the cargo on the patrol car. "Lehman, you guys need to go, get him back to the Terminal before he bleeds out."

"We all need to go," Ryan said.

"I can't. There's something I have to do," Hinds replied.

He pulled rifle ammunition from the back of the aircraft to replenish his kit. "My wife has a house not far from Syracuse. If she's there, then this is my last chance to save my child."

"I have orders to take all of you back to the Terminal. I can't let you leave. I'm sorry."

"You have orders to bring the cargo back. The rest of us don't matter." Lehman threw her weapon over her shoulder and joined Hinds in the patrol car. "I'm going with you." Ryan stared at her, silent and disappointed, unwilling to leave her behind.

"When I leave, no one else is coming for you, Paige."

"We'll find our own way back."

Ryan walked away reluctantly, boarded the aircraft, and took off with the others for the Terminal. It was quiet now, with Elnath rising slowly over 189's horizon and painting the sky a dim red. Off in the distance, Those For tanks could be clearly seen moving back into the city.

"You should have gone with them."

"I'll never abandon you again, Hinds." She climbed into the gunner's seat and loaded the mini-gun. "We'll be found soon if we don't get moving."

And so they went, alone, far behind enemy lines toward one more uncertain objective.

***

"She's home. I can see the light on in the living room." Hinds observed his old residence from the cover of tall brush nearby. It hadn't changed. The small one-story house was untouched by the war. "You think she'll be in there alone?"

"Doesn't matter. One way or another, we're leaving with the baby."

"She'll never agree to that."

"We didn't come this far to negotiate."

Hinds looked over at her as she watched the house through her optics. She was right. There was no room for negotiation. If they left the baby here, it was dead.

"There's movement," she said. Hinds looked through his optics and saw the figures of a man and woman walking through the living room toward a couch. "Seems she hasn't wasted any time. How do you wanna play this, Hinds?"

"I'm not sure." He thought of using brute force, but it would be minutes before a T.F. patrol arrived and apprehended them. "There are three rooms in the house: The kitchen, which is right by the front door, the living room, and the bedroom. If you can get them to the front door, I can search for the baby."

"How do you know they won't have the baby with them?"

"I don't, but they were walking away from the bedroom, where I'm hoping they left it, asleep. "

Lehman packed away her optics. "We can't mess this up, you know. One mistake here, and that's it."

"I've pulled us out of worse situations before."

"All of which you got us into in the first place. If there is any sign that they've spotted you, I'm killing your wife and whoever she's with." She drew her weapon, checked for ammunition, and placed it back in its holster.

"You'll have to explain that to the baby when it gets older."

"I'll say you made me shoot them. Don't get caught."

Hinds low-crawled through the bushes over to the bedroom window and signaled to Lehman that he was ready. Taking a deep breath, she rose from the ground and walked as calmly as she could down the path to the front door of the house. Surprisingly, the pair inside seemed unaware of her as she passed by the living room window.

She arrived at the house and knocked at the door as loudly as she could. The faint sound of laughter inside ceased and was quickly followed by footsteps making their approach. Lehman hoped Hinds had a good line of sight through the bedroom window because there was no way of letting him know the coast was clear.

A short, pulpy man answered the door.

"Can I help you?" he asked. Lehman quickly glanced behind him and saw the women walking toward them.

"I'm here to speak with a woman named Nicole regarding her husband."

"I am her husband." There was anger in his tone, but it brought no concern, as he clearly wasn't built for confrontation.

"Then by order of Those For, you're under arrest," she lied. "We have reason to believe you were involved in a recent attack against one of our facilities."

"I think you're referring to my ex," the woman interrupted, coming forward as the man stepped aside, taken aback by the statement. "My name is Nicole." She was tall and beautiful. Lehman found it hard to believe that she would set her standards so low for a replacement spouse. "Please, come in."

She followed her into the kitchen, and the two studied one another in silence for a while. Around them, Lehman found personal effects from what must have been a very recent wedding, as well as photos of a baby girl hanging on the walls.

"Are you aware your former husband is working with Those Against?"

"It's why we split. Whatever he's doing out there now has nothing to do with me. He left a long time ago." She moved over to her stove and grabbed a kettle. "Would you like tea?"

"Please." She watched her in feigned disbelief at her reply. "Why should I believe you aren't conspiring against us with him?"

"For what reason?" the pulpy man replied, sitting down at their kitchen table. Lehman ignored him and kept her eyes on Nicole, who remained unmoved by her doubt as she filled a cup with hot water.

"My parents funded the sphere." Lehman's hands trembled softly as she took the cup from her adversary. Her family was responsible for this entire conflict. She took a sip of tea and contemplated how long it would take patrols to arrive at the house if she were to kill both of them right now and make a run for it. Just then, the faint sound of a window closing could be heard coming from the bedroom, signaling her partner's escape. "Though I assume you and the rest of Those For already know that," she continued.

"Of course. Still, we have to be sure." Lehman placed her cup on the table and turned toward the door, keeping her eyes on the pair as they stood to escort her out. "I trust you'll report to the authorities if you hear from him?"

They nodded and led her outside. As the door closed behind her, she took off, walking quickly toward the patrol car parked at the end of the road. She was careful not to draw suspicion by running, though at any moment, they could realize the baby was missing and call for help.

She found Hinds hiding on the floor of the car, holding the baby in his arms, and watched her as she stared back at them in silent curiosity. Miraculously, the girl hadn't made a sound, despite having been woken abruptly from her sleep.

"Let's go home." Lehman started the car and began the long drive back toward friendly lines. Hours passed before the pair arrived at a crossing where the main engagement had taken place the previous night. The remains of destroyed equipment and the bodies of T.A. soldiers were scattered all around. T.F. slaughtered them to the last man. The light infantry dispatched by COL Deeley never stood a chance against enemy tanks, but they were all he could spare without sacrificing the Terminal.

"They're all from the twenty-seventh," Lehman said. She found the familiar unit insignia on the shoulders of the bodies that were still intact and tried not to picture the faces of the friends she knew were there. Hinds covered his daughter's eyes to save her from any memory of the scene before them and said a prayer for the deceased. He wondered if anyone from Delta Company had escaped this time.

As they neared T.A's forward line, the baby began to cry, breaking the silence she had maintained for the entire trip just as they were out of danger. Hinds held her close, unsure of what else he could do.

"Was it wrong to take her from her mother?" he asked.

"She still has a mother." Lehman slowed the car to a stop and left the driver's seat. "I need a break. Switch with me?"

Hinds cautiously passed the child to her and traded positions. Immediately, the girl calmed down.

"Have you named her yet?"

Hinds shook his head. He hadn't even considered that under the pressure of the last few days.

"Brynhildr. It means 'armored fighting woman.'" She looked down at the baby as though seeking her approval and was met with a tiny smile. Hinds stared at them without saying a word as he admired his friend and his daughter—their daughter, in what would likely be the last peaceful moment they would ever have.

IX

THE INFINITE ENEMY

CDR Cochran forced herself across the Terminal for the second time that day to check on the fleet's progress. The Terminal hangar had been hastily expanded to accommodate the ships that would take humanity away from 189, and her newly recruited staff wasted no time in their construction. In the four months following the battle, they had built fifty ships, five rows of ten lining the room, with the largest of each at the very end, built to carry passengers.

She made her way to the end of the third row and stopped at the fleet's prized ship, the *Beacon of Hope*. Massive and unnecessarily extravagant as it was, it still wasn't enough. Nothing here ever would be. She knew she could ferry ten-thousand souls away from the planet at best, and there were, unfortunately, far greater numbers fighting for admission at the gates.

"One launch," Anirban said behind her. She looked back at him faintly bemused but said nothing. "We can afford one launch at near-C speeds with the anti-matter the kids brought back. There isn't enough to start again once we stop."

"I know. Dr. Pajares and Dr. Yizar are on the Foundation reviewing our chosen trajectory."

"The demon will consume Elnath until it is no more and search the universe inexorably for energy until destroyed. It is the Infinite Enemy." Anirban traced his hand along the warp drive affixed to the Beacon's fuselage. "When we activate this in concert with the others, the burst of energy will rival that of a solar flare. If the machines give chase before we're at peak speed, we won't escape."

"I'll have my team come up with a plan to outpace—or at least delay them until we're clear. It's someone else's problem to figure out how to beat them…future leaders, perhaps. All we can do now is run and hope." CDR Cochran closed her eyes and listened to the clamor of worker bees running to and fro, assembling the last remaining pieces of the fleet. She tried to imagine 189 outside the Terminal, to feel its tall grass beneath her feet and the fresh surface air inside her lungs. It occurred to her that very soon, she and all the others would trade the nature they took for granted for a cold, artificial life aboard these ships. She held herself there, silent in her mental retreat, oblivious to the chaos around her until the sound of crashing metal brought her to, and her eyes opened to a warp drive, fallen to the ground from its damaged holsters.

***

Dr. Pajares studied Elnath from his seat on the *Foundation*'s observation deck while Dr. Yizar, the station's only other occupant, monitored his console. The star itself was nearly invisible, entombed within a sphere of surrounding machines, its light shining only briefly through small gaps on its surface. Jorge wondered what had become of 189 as it sat in total darkness.

By now, whatever fighting there was still left to do would either be at its end or winding down. Any further engagements at this point served no purpose. By now, everyone on the surface would know that life there was no longer sustainable. Opponents and supporters alike would make last-minute attempts to reach the Terminal, where they would inevitably discover that there wasn't enough room to hold everyone inside. They would surely fight to the death for access, only to find even less room in the fleet.

He decided he would leave the problem of admission to the commander and the leaders on the ground. She had left him with a much bigger issue: That of creating a delay. Evidently, there was some concern that the machines would shift their focus to the escaping fleet, and current data seemed to support that theory.

"Ilides," Dr. Yizar said, beckoning Jorge to one of the screens at his console. "They're starting to break away toward Ilides."

Jorge transferred Ebon's video feed to the deck's central display and focused it on the star's lower-right quadrant. There he found a single trail of probes, machines much larger than those surrounding Elnath, flying to and from its closest planet.

"What's going on there?"

"I'm not sure. I've never seen probes like that."

The observers followed the machines as they traveled from the planet back to the swarm and realized that they returned in groups to separate hubs—probes even larger than themselves for docking.

"Seems like they're not just replicating. They're improving. They can cover great distances now."

"I suppose they'll devour everything then."

"As expected." Jorge kept his eyes on Elnath and wondered if this scenario was playing itself out anywhere else in the universe. He thought of other stars fading from the night sky, questioning whether their light went out naturally or if some civilization had made the same error. Perhaps this was a regular occurrence, the Great Filter's next step. Perhaps many others before them had encountered a similar fate and were prisoners, slaves, and hunted adversaries of their own creations. If it wasn't a pandemic, nuclear warfare, or some natural disaster that led them to extinction, he supposed it had to be this. "We still owe her a trajectory."

"And a plan to delay those beasts outside. Kelsey asks a lot of us."

"She shoulders a heavy weight. We're just here to help her carry it. You and I and all the others." Jorge pulled out a copy of CDR Cochran's most recent directive and panned the central display out over Elnath's entire system. "Once that drive starts up, the burst of energy will be a feast for those probes, compared to what's left of the star."

"It should only be a short burst. Maybe it won't last long enough to attract any attention."

"And maybe it will—think worst-case scenario. This plan has no room for optimism. Assuming we're able to get the fleet into orbit before the horde triples its rate of expansion, how much time do you suppose we'll need?"

"However long it takes to mass the fleet above 189, guide it to the starting point of whatever trajectory we decide and push the drive to maximum speed. Assuming worst-case, of course, that each of those events attracts attention, I'd say thirty minutes." Both men diligently traced the probes' route between Elnath and Ilides with the shared understanding that the machines would reach them long before that.

"What if we create a separate burst in between the drones and 189?" Jorge asked. Ebon turned to his monitor, searched through his files, and opened another set of projections on the central display.

"I had thought about that earlier, but it presents us with another set of issues." This time, he rose from his seat and took control of the display, centering the projection on the point exactly halfway between Elnath and 189. "First, how do we produce a burst energetic enough to distract them from the drive? The resources available to create such explosives will either have been expended during the war or allocated to the fleet." He paused for a short while, as though expecting an immediate solution from his counterpart, but received nothing. "Then, how do we know exactly where to put it in order to give us the maximum time to escape and avoid damaging anything in the fleet?"

Ebon simulated an explosion on display near a small fleet about one-third the size of the one they were hoping to launch. In the projection, the burst of energy shifted the fleet just slightly off its path, no matter where he positioned it.

"A small explosion pushed this fleet thirty kilometers away from its course. That may seem marginal at first, but it could eventually cause us to miss star systems that we otherwise would have hit—and remember, we can't adjust." Still, Jorge said nothing, only continuing to stare at the projection and occasionally glance, in thought, around the room.

"Even if we get all of that right," Ebon went on, "how will we know for sure that it will give us enough time?"

Finally, Jorge returned to his seat and spoke. "I've never been much good at math, so I'll let you work that out. As for the burst," he pointed behind him to the door that led into the observation deck and out toward the *Foundation*'s reactor, "we'll use the station."

***

The names of those killed in T.A's final engagement flashed across a screen at Central Terminal that formerly displayed arrival and departure times. One hundred columns of thirty names on the board: three-thousand soldiers of the 27th Infantry Regiment fallen on the battlegrounds of Syracuse at first count. An entire echelon wiped out, with more names to follow, surely, in the days to come.

Hinds waited in front of the screen with his daughter and read the list of names, vainly hoping not to find any he recognized. Within seconds, he found the name of a Delta Company Soldier who he'd only met briefly in the trenches on the island. Then, he found more from his outfit: SSG Adkins, LT Negron, CPT Sullivan and SGT Radd. They lingered in place for a moment too short for him to react and moved on. Another minute brought another page of names, and this time, he found COL Deeley, the last name he could bear to see.

A hand on his shoulder took his attention away from the board—it was Lehman, returning from her shift at the gate. She read along for only a short while before she spoke. As she did, the baby opened her eyes and reached for her.

"My turn," she said, exchanging her weapon for Brynn and her duty as a guard for caretaker. "Traffic at the gate is much worse today. Something like twice as many people out there."

"You think Nicole made her way down?"

"Doesn't matter. The fleet's at capacity, according to Cochran. No one else is getting in."

Hinds worried again for Brynn, who bounced carefree in her new mother's arms, indifferent to her current circumstances and the loss of her old one. "That's a shame."

"You don't need her anyway, but you do need to get outside. The 45th Brigade doesn't have enough guards. I think they're starting to fill their ranks with civvies who've already made it through."

Hinds nodded, looked at the two together briefly, and departed for the Terminal gates.

"Safe tour," Lehman said before strapping the baby into the harness on her chest and leaving herself in search of the commander.

The halls of the Terminal, normally congested with personnel, were nearly vacant since all available hands were either on guard or loading supplies and equipment onto the fleet. Lehman made her way across the lower level and through the warren, eventually passing by the former chambers of COL Deeley.

It stood empty now, entirely devoid of books, paperwork, and wall decor. Even his loyal staff members who often seemed to take up residence here had disbanded—perhaps leaving their work behind to race for the best possible accommodations aboard the fleet. She paused momentarily to read the large inscription carved into the wall behind his desk, *Audeamus - Let Us Dare*, and continued on.

Lehman found the commander alone at the centrifuge, oblivious to her entrance as she stared at the machine. It had been stripped down to bare wiring for parts and hung in the center of the room like a skeleton on display. The glass panels that previously surrounded the structure and separated it from the observation deck were absent, leaving the room a vast open space that remained silent until broken by the baby's echoing coo.

"And who might that be?" CDR Cochran said, awoken from her trance. She approached the pair and leaned over for a closer look at the child.

"Hinds' daughter."

"She's precious. May I hold her?"

"You can try," Lehman replied, pulling the baby from the harness and handing her over, amidst a loud cry and a flurry of tears.

"Shhh. It's okay, sweet baby." The commander took the child and returned to the centrifuge, with Lehman close in tow. "Where's her father?"

"He just replaced me at the gate." Cochran continued to rock the baby gently in her arms, trying to avoid Lehman's eyes and any discussion of the events unfolding outside. "People are getting violent out there."

"We can't save everyone. We may not even save ourselves. This plan, in all likelihood, is suicide." As she spoke, the chamber doors opened to reveal Anirban Acharya quickly approaching them, his stride momentarily disrupted by the presence of the unfamiliar child. He nodded at her and delivered his message.

"The fleet is ready to go."

"Are you sure?"

Anirban remained silent, the feigned confidence generally apparent on his face absent, for what Kelsey felt was the first time. The commander handed the baby back to her mother, and the four of them headed toward the staged fleet.

"We'll need to wait for them to get in position before we launch. How long until green light?"

"Two hours."

"Make the boarding call and get those civilians loaded up wherever they'll fit."

"And the gate guards?"

"Bring them in and seal the Terminal doors. Those should hold off the crowd until departure."

Anirban acknowledged his orders and split from them down a separate path through the Warren toward Central Terminal.

"Green light? What are we waiting for?" Lehman asked. The commander trailed a short distance ahead of her, unaware that she had stopped.

"For the Foundation to move in between us and the drones."

"We still have people up there."

"I know," she replied, with her back turned. "They're buying us time to launch."

Cochran stared firmly at the tiles on the ground as the two officers stood in silence. She anticipated the next question and knew Lehman would not accept her answer.

"At green light, the station will be postured to self-destruct and lure the drones away with a nuclear blast. The procedure can only be initiated from onboard, so Ebon and

Jorge…they'll have to stay behind." She felt the captain's gaze without looking back at her. She was choosing to abandon her friends, who had risked more than any other civilian on 189 to provide them this one final chance to survive, and in the end, their reward would be a violent death in the cold abyss of space.

"They don't deserve that," Lehman replied, passing her judgment without hesitation.

"Their souls will rest among the billions I've sacrificed to save just a small piece of humanity. There is no other way, and they know it. One day, if you're ever in command, maybe you'll see." Kelsey left Lehman in the Warren and proceeded alone toward the staging area, where she would make the hardest decision ever made by anyone in all of human history.

***

The crowds charged the gates as guards were pulled back, and the Terminal doors began to close. A voice shouted orders over the facility's intercom, instructing soldiers on the line to break away from their posts in waves to prevent them from being immediately overrun. From his position at the relatively quiet southeast gate, Hinds could hear bursts of gunfire and frantic screams coming from both sides as guards shot down civilians who tried to get through.

In front of him now was a gathering of about thirty people standing completely still and watching his formation in silence. Their previous attempt at storming this gate a day prior had failed, with more than one hundred souls torn from their ranks by guards under the command of a ruthless watch officer. There was talk around the Terminal indicating that the watch officer was CPT Harris, the commander who had fled here to safety after going AWOL during their battle at AO Baker. Hinds forced her out of his mind—he wouldn't fire a single round at a civilian, of that he was sure, even if his watch officer ordered him to.

Guards at the southeast gate were spread out evenly in one line, ten soldiers deep between the rails on either side of their post. At the center of the formation and nearest the large hangar door leading into the facility, a young man was waiting at an angle, with his body pointing almost directly at the structure behind him as though, at any moment, he would abandon his duty and run. Four soldiers to his right was another, holding his weapon at the low-ready, his finger in the trigger well, and a first target already decided as he stared back at the crowd with sweat dripping down his face.

The intensity of the protest at various sections of the gate seemed to magnify ten-fold once alarms sounded at the close of each hangar door, putting everyone on edge. It wasn't long before the chaos of the alarms reached the southeast corridor, ripping through the quiet standoff on both sides, with the crowd beginning to push aggressively toward the fence once again, stumbling over one another as they advanced.

After only a short few steps forward, an object came barreling through the air toward Hinds, who was unable to identify what it was. From afar, no one could clearly see it, and when the soldier with his weapon at the ready assumed it to be an explosive, he retaliated accordingly. Before the projectile even hit the ground and before anyone could object, he discharged his weapon into the crowd, which stopped for a moment to find its sole casualty: A child who had thrown her favorite doll over the fence in an attempt to save it from mankind's greatest adversary.

When the doll landed at Hinds' feet, all hell broke loose. People in the crowd darted over the fence now with no regard for those around them nor their own safety. Groups of five or more vaulted themselves over the barbed wire and onto the guards who were already running for their lives toward the hangar. The lieutenant was lost briefly in a daze as he stared at the doll on the ground. It was a penguin in a camouflage uniform. He picked it up with the intention of throwing it back but realized there was no one to receive it. Its owner had perished as an innocent victim of a meaningless war.

With only seconds to spare, he turned and ran for the door, narrowly clearing the gap between the steel pillars forcing themselves closed. Then, they shut, silencing the uproar of the condemned civilians outside and cutting them away from humanity forever. Central Terminal provided little reprieve, as the scene inside mirrored the chaos that Hinds had just escaped. In every direction, people pushed and shoved their way across the facility, searching for their loved ones, grabbing hold of whatever belongings they had, and running for the ships. Their time on 189 was up.

"Lieutenant, come with me!" It was Anirban Acharya, shouting at him from across the floor, barely audible over the commotion. Hinds forced his way through the crowd, still clutching the doll's arm as though it were the little girl who threw it. "The others are already on the Beacon."

"What's going on?"

"We need to leave right now. Anyone not on board a carrier in the next thirty minutes won't be making this trip.

Hurry, please, quickly." The old man led him down a maze of hallways back toward the staging area, where the panic continued. Here, there were long, disorganized lines formed next to four of the five carriers. Armed guards surrounded the fifth.

When they approached the final carrier, Anirban pulled a badge from his collar and flashed it at the two soldiers blocking the ramp, who immediately parted to grant them access. Hinds looked over his shoulder at the confusion beneath them as they climbed aboard, aware that he'd likely just taken the last steps he ever would outside of a ship.

"Welcome to the Beacon of Hope." Anirban seemed to relax now, and he took the seat closest to CDR Cochran, who was already monitoring displays at the ship's helm. "This is the bridge whe—"

"Where are the others?" Hinds ignored Anirban and directed his question at the commander. Cochran glanced at him briefly before shifting her attention to the live stream of the boarding process in front of her.

"Chief," she said, speaking to one of the operators seated at a separate console. "Please escort the lieutenant to his quarters. His family is expecting him." The operator stood and exited down a path behind the bridge, pausing momentarily to ensure his charge followed. Cochran knew that his family wasn't who he was referring to, as concerned about them as he may be. Directly below her center console were two vacant seats reserved for the scientists who should have already been there.

She watched the lieutenant depart with his eyes fixed on her as he left, knowing she would be held liable for all of this later.

The Beacon itself was unnecessarily extravagant, clearly built to house a certain demographic: The aristocracy of 189. Its wide passageways were lined with living quarters spacious enough to house two or three families each, yet Hinds could see open rooms occupied by single individuals as he was brought to his own at the back end of the hall. Perpendicular to his room on either side were paths that stretched out infinitely toward sections still under development, making the carrier seem much larger inside than was physically possible. The lack of personnel onboard compared to other ships compounded the illusion. Their new society had already made its first mistake—the establishment of a privileged class. Personnel on the Beacon would travel in relative comfort while all the others suffered the close quarters of their fellow man.

The operator entered a code into a panel on the door, and seconds later, it opened to reveal Ryan and Paige together with his daughter. They had been speaking about him, no doubt, since their conversation ceased upon his entry.

"I'll give you two some time." Ryan placed her hand on Lehman's shoulder and left to join the command team. When the doors closed behind her, Hinds moved quietly next to the baby, who was fast asleep in a small pram adjacent to the carrier's rear porthole. Behind her, the two officers had a clear view of the fleet. With ten minutes remaining until the green light, the hangar was empty. Everyone who had made it inside the Terminal was slated to a carrier, and there was nothing left on the planet to do.

"Did she tell you about Ebon and Jorge?" Lehman asked, breaking the silence. "They're sacrificing themselves."

She received no response, and both continued staring forward and away from one another. Something about this encounter—something in the air told Hinds what was coming. After a short while, Lehman reached underneath her collar, pulled the chain from her neck, and held it aloft.

"Hinds, thank you for everything, but I can't accept this."

He turned toward her now and stepped back, assaulted by the sight of the ring that dangled at its end. At the very same moment, a violent tremor shook the Terminal as the hangar ascended toward its ceiling, startling the baby awake.

"Green light in five," sounded the intercom.

Up above, the walls parted in preparation for launch. And the engines around the ship sparked to life with such fury that the chain fell from Lehman's hand and onto the floor beneath them. Brynn burst into tears and reached for her mother when the ring touched the ground but missed her, as Lehman had already started for the door.

"I'm sorry," she said, looking over her shoulder at him one last time before exiting the room to find that he had tears in his eyes too.

***

"One minute to departure." CPT Lehman arrived at the bridge just as the commander made her final warning and sat two rows behind the center console. She attracted very little attention from the operators, who were fully concentrated on the launch. They had no room for error here. "Everyone strap in."

Her fiancée was seated where Jorge would have been, were he not on the *Foundation*. She found Ryan looking back at her, hoping for a sign that she had cut her counterpart out of the picture. With a simple nod, Lehman broke away and immersed herself in more immediate matters, subconsciously placing her hand where the ring had been.

The *Beacon of Hope* was off the ground now, hovering at an angle one-hundred meters above the Terminal gates. Behind it in a wedge formation were the four remaining carriers: *Quaker Ridge*, *Manhattan*, *St. Robert*, and *Mount Vernon*, each with its cargo vessels in tow. Lehman felt herself press against her seat under the force of gravity as the ship jolted forward.

Through the noise of the engines, she was faintly able to hear the familiar sound of Kelsey Cochran counting them down into uncertainty over the intercom, as she had done with their orbital drop not long ago. She watched the commander she had judged, calm under mental and physical pressure, and forgave her for sacrificing so many lives to bring them here.

At this critical moment, it was clear that Cochran was the right officer in the right place, at the right time to save humanity. Despite everything, she was the greatest of their generation.

As her discomfort grew with the ever-increasing force, Lehman's mind drifted away to irrelevant places. She thought of the little bar in New Rochelle and wondered if McGregor ever made it to safety. She thought of her parents and whether or not they had survived the occupation that had trapped them in Wurzburg.

Then she thought of Brynn and hoped that her father had secured her properly against the effects of the launch. The image of the crying baby almost tore her from her harness, but under the current conditions, she knew better. After an indeterminate period of time, the carrier was in orbit, and Lehman's body was free from nature's grasp.

"Anirban, start the drive." The old man activated two of the three levers at his console required to complete initiation but hesitated at the third, knowing that the moment he pulled it, the scientists were dead.

Radar systems on the bridge sounded an alert indicating a shift in the direction of the drones surrounding Ilides. The swarm had detected them and was en route. Drone hubs trailed behind their subordinate probes toward the pulsating energy created by the bubble's startup, quickly bypassing other dead planets between Elnath and the *Foundation*, which sat in position to defend. Anirban forced himself to pull the final lever, as any further delay would cost them their escape.

A burst of light temporarily blinded the crew as the bubble encased the fleet. It was so bright that Lehman could count the bones in the arm she used to cover her eyes. She was the last to recover, regaining her sight just as objects outside began to distort themselves into thin red lines. Beneath the ship Corina-189, the birthplace of all they knew, faded into a blur at the corner of the Beacon's viewport before anyone aboard could see it.

Not far from it, Elnath lay fully exposed at a fraction of its former luminosity as the drones pulled away. Hinds, in his quarters now at the rear of the ship, would be watching behind them while the others faced ahead. He would look upon their home star one final time and know, more than anyone else, how brilliant the sun of 189 once was.

After a few seconds, the only thing the crew on the bridge could distinguish outside the bubble was another flash, this one further away. The blast that produced it shut down the ship's systems for a while, but as they came back online, they realized that the Infinite Enemy had slowed, redirected toward a new, more immediate target.

CDR Cochran stood first once the drive was steady, rendering a salute to the *Foundation* and its small crew that had traded their lives to buy them just enough time. Around her, the remainder of her team joined in silent respect to their fallen partners—all except for one. In the back of the room, Paige Lehman kept her seat and focused her attention on the radar, where a handful of drones could be seen following them at a distance out of the star system and into the abyss.

PART II - PRESENT

I

GOODBYE TO ALL THAT

Brynn pushed her way through the Beacon's crowded atrium and felt as though its walls were quickly closing in on her. Seventeen years here and still, she remained an outcast amongst the socialites and a stranger to the day-to-day activities of their class—despite her parents 'status. This was the *Beacon of Hope*, after all, the very first ship built on the colony. It was the center of everything, and no expense had been spared in its development. Her privilege afforded her an escape from the less-than-acceptable conditions shared by passengers on neighboring ships, but it couldn't prevent her from finding trouble of her own.

Behind her in close pursuit were members of the Council, chasing after her for an object she shouldn't have: a handheld radio that enabled communication with other carriers. Off-ship comms were allowed, though strictly controlled at the highest levels of government, but never restricted entirely. Not like this. The Council had locked away this specific radio for reasons unknown to Brynn. She had to know why, and that meant she had to have it.

She picked up her pace and scanned behind her for her partner, who had helped her steal it, only to find the out-of-place figures slithering like snakes through the crowd. There were three of them, or at least three that she could find, cutting in and out of view so quickly that she felt they weren't real.

Where was her friend?

Gone away to safety, perhaps?

Didn't matter. She knew that other assailants could be anywhere, waiting in ambush directly ahead of her.

After ten minutes of chase, Brynn cut left down a perpendicular hallway at a near-sprint toward her mother's working quarters, where she knew they wouldn't dare follow. She arrived to a set of steel doors at its entrance and waited, watching the guilty reflection on its surface stare back at her with a shared understanding that this particular visit could not end well.

Sensing approaching footsteps, she entered an override code into the panel on the door and ran through, instantly regretting her decision as she met the eyes of Lieutenant General Lehman at the far end of the room.

Brynn made the endless walk toward her demise without looking away, preparing the best possible lie to convey her innocence to a woman she knew would not be fooled. To her dismay, General Lehman sat at her desk in conference with five Council guards watching a video feed of two figures leaving a restricted area, one of whom was dressed the same as her, with an object hidden beneath her coat. The evidence was damning.

"I'd expect a thief to be more aware of her surroundings. Especially when there are cameras directly above her mark." She pointed at Brynn's coat without waiting for a response, and the girl turned over the radio to her without giving one. "Your father will be disappointed."

"What'll it matter to me? He's never here." She wished immediately that she hadn't said anything.

In the brief silence that followed, it occurred to her that this was the first time she had ever seen the two apart. General Lehman and her father had been the closest of friends for decades, having essentially saved humanity at her age. Of course, they would both be disappointed in her, the problem child, the delinquent, the thief.

"Your behavior is unnecessarily reckless. What could you possibly need this for?"

"To escape. To reach out and touch someone real, someone outside the Beacon. This ship is killing me!"

"No one is choosing to stay onboard, but there are no other options. The people who live here, they've been planet-side. They were raised there. Do you think you want an escape more than them? We run because we can't fight. There is no plan to engage our enemy, and you have no plan nor the resolve to face the Council should they prosecute you for misconduct."

Brynn said nothing and only stood in silent embarrassment staring at the cold frame of the carrier. She was never able to walk on 189, nor did she remember anything about it.

All she knew was this.

A minute later, the general rose to her feet, signaling the end of their meeting. "I've called the guards away, but let this happen again, and I'll personally hand-deliver you to trial."

"Understood, ma'am."

"You're dismissed."

Brynn rendered a salute and returned under escort by her mother's guards to her quarters. For the time being, she would do as she was told.

Lehman took the radio, examined it closely, and turned the dial on its side to a specific frequency. This particular device had been confiscated by the Council for its ability to send encrypted messages. After checking behind her at the door to ensure the room was empty, she engaged the transmitter and spoke.

"Anirban, we're back online."

***

Hours later, Brynn tossed restlessly in her bed, dreaming of imprisonment aboard an oxygen-deficient cargo ship, waiting for her inevitable execution. The reality of her dream shook her awake to an empty quarters.

As expected, her father wasn't there, gone to one of his usual early work calls. She laid still for a while, not yet entirely conscious, facing the ceiling and listening to the quiet buzz of the Beacon's engine.

The clock near the door read 0400—two hours before her classes were scheduled to start. Beneath it was a packed lunch and an equally expected handwritten note for her, probably outlining the reason behind her father's latest absence. Had he been around more often, he'd have known that she rarely attended school, as the general lack of upward mobility aboard the fleet made the institution pointless. The only reason she would make the effort today was to show her mother a sincere attempt to stay in line.

"Another long day," she said.

She rose and shifted her line of sight toward the porthole at the rear of her quarters. Over the years, the view from its massive porthole at her bedside had not changed much, as the stars made little adjustment against the endless backdrop of space, especially at such slow speeds. Through it, she searched for the Impact Zone and quickly found the familiar dark cloud in the sky—Impact Elnath, or (I) Elnath for short. After their malfunction, the drones that made up the Dyson Sphere surrounding their home star broke away and devoured all energy in the solar system along with the surrounding systems in every direction. Because of the perpetual nature of its expansion and the speed at which it moved, (I) Elnath could always be seen from The *Beacon of Hope*, regardless of how far it moved away.

In its current state, the colony couldn't consider stopping to find a replacement world for Corina-189, not with this evil endlessly chasing them. That was an undeniable fact, one that Brynn knew was on the mind of every individual on every ship, whether or not they admitted it.

Even with her limited knowledge of astrophysics and propulsion mechanics, she knew there was only so far that they could run, as the Alcubierre Drive, which served as their ferry, was not moving the colony fast enough to travel extreme distances.

At just over the speed of light, the nearest galaxy outside her own Milky Way would still take more than two million years to reach. *If (I) Elnath doesn't stop expanding before we leave the galaxy, what then? Extinction?*

Suddenly, her train of thought was broken by the sound of the buzzer.

"Who is it?" she asked, unaware of how much time had passed.

"It's Coleman. Are you ready?"

Don Coleman was one of the very few friends Brynn had in the entire colony. She quickly threw on her uniform and ran outside to meet him and her mandatory escort.

"Well, someone's on lockdown, he teased, handing her a cup of coffee. "I'm guessing things didn't go well with your mom."

"What gave that away?" The pair headed for the university block, paying no mind to the three guards in tow. "Have the other students been talking about it?"

"Everyone. Word around campus is that you'll be expelled. Is that true? What did your mom say?"

"No, not true. At least not for that—for truancy, maybe. She didn't say anything serious."

They made their way toward the far end of the hall and turned into the second door on the left, where they found an empty classroom. 0558, a little bit early. Brynn thought, glancing down at her watch.

At the door, the guards remained, to her continued embarrassment. Both students took their seats in the front row and waited, but after fifteen minutes, no one, not even their instructor, had arrived. She looked over at Coleman, who had the same expression of concern strewn across his face. It couldn't be a coincidence that both aggressors from the previous day were here under armed guard.

Just as the reality of their situation became apparent, the guards outside burst into the classroom, their size tripled from that of the escort who brought them here. With them was General Lehman, standing with arms crossed as her legion encircled them.

"Nothing serious, huh?" The moment Coleman spoke, the impact from a baton on his shoulder forced him to the ground.

"Don!" Brynn screamed before another guard shoved her to the ground next to him. In an instant, both were restrained.

"There seems to be an issue of discipline aboard this ship," Lehman said, crouching beside her daughter. "One stemming from a wish to escape. Since you've failed to appreciate your home on the Beacon, I've decided to grant you that wish."

She resumed an upright posture and began to exit the classroom, turning back toward them just as she reached the door.

"As of this morning, you've been reassigned to Mount Vernon until further notice. By order of the commanding general."

Brynn fought to push the guard away and regain control, but a fierce kick to the stomach silenced her. As her vision dimmed to a blur from the pain, she cursed her parents, begging in vain for them not to send her away, but she was too late. Ahead of her now, General Lehman abandoned them—they had no choice but to execute her father's orders.

***

Brynn regained consciousness, seated inside an oscillating vault with her hands still tied behind her back and no sense of any passage of time. With great difficulty, she tried to shift her body around to examine her surroundings but was held stationary by additional restraints on her torso and legs. Through a small glass panel across from her, she could see open space and the very top of what she thought was a ship. As the vault rotated, the ship tilted into view, and the words *Beacon of Hope* appeared across its hull. She realized that the room she was in must be part of a transport en route to the *Mount Vernon*, and the carrier outside was her home.

A voice startled her from the opposite side of the thin metal wall behind her. "Seems pretty serious to me." It was Coleman, restrained just the same.

"Don. I'm sorry."

"For what? How many of our classmates do you think have seen the Beacon from outside?"

None.

No one her age would have any idea how immense the carrier truly was, let alone the fleet. Confinement in their space-borne cell had provided them the gift of perspective. All they had ever known was right there. Their portion of human history hovered beneath them, flying amongst other ships of varying sizes in a tight formation. Brynn could even trace the bubble, the mythical shell that kept them together and made them complete. Outside, she found the infinite universe and the Infinite Enemy in its familiar pursuit.

Within minutes, their short-lived reverence came to an end, and the transport slammed against the docking bay of the Mount. Inside, both were shaken violently as clamps on either side of the hull locked them in place. Guards from the foreign carrier met them at its entrance shortly afterward, pulling Coleman away first and dragging him by the arm out of the transport. Then they came for Brynn, who was nearly lifted off her feet as she was carried out onto the first tier.

The Mount was in a state of considerable disrepair, with clear evidence of damage to its frame visible from inside. Fixtures bearing shattered lights and dents folding inwards lined the interior as though there had been great impacts on the ship's hull. Many of the carbon dioxide scrubbers placed at intervals along the walls and ceiling were filled to capacity with the black sludge known to pile up when they weren't properly cleaned. Doors at various sections of the tier were sealed to prevent civilians from being vented into space, as the rooms behind them had been.

Brynn and Coleman fell in line at a checkpoint immediately outside the docking bay, behind other passengers waiting to be screened for entry—all of whom suffered the physical toll of oxygen deficiency. Guards ahead checked them both for concealed weapons and led them through the central corridors of the first tier toward an unknown destination.

The *Mount Vernon* differed significantly from the Beacon in terms of structure: Society on this ship was separated into five tiers, with conditions deteriorating exponentially at the lower levels. Everything from food rations to electricity and heat was divvied out to passengers on a top-down basis. Priority went to the administrators on the first two tiers, while scraps were sent to all the others below.

Brynn squeezed through the growing crowds as carefully as she could, following her escorts closely past the watchful eyes of natives unused to the presence of foreigners aboard their carrier. Eventually, their group arrived at an elevator and followed a single guard inside until they were packed in. Then they began their descent, slowly passing by the second and third tiers and screeching to a halt on the fourth.

By the time they stopped, half of their party lay prone on the floor of the lift, faint from the increasingly difficult task of breathing. Those who could stand were directed out into a maze of winding corridors with four-person rooms arranged in stacks of two and led to their quarters and separated by gender.

***

A bitter cold draft flowing through the quarters Brynn shared with three other women shook them all to their feet at 0400 the following morning. They were left there with no food and only the clothes on their backs to keep them warm. Brynn spent the entire night prior on high alert, leaning against a wall at the corner of the room, watching her bunkmates and hoping they didn't attack her. They were transfers from other carriers that also must not have fared well since all three women looked as though they wore the same clothing that they boarded with almost twenty years ago.

An alarm sounded as one of them tried to exit the quarters, attracting the attention of a guard on patrol not far from their room. He banged on the metal grate on their locked door, ordered the four occupants back against the far wall, and then entered to address them.

"My name is Captain Alexander Hernandez, Commander of the Mount."

He quickly inspected each of them, pulled out a paper list, and began reading off their individual tier assignments. The first woman was assigned to the second tier for her experience in refrigeration unit repair. The next two were former convicts, recently set free from a prison cargo ship, and both assigned to this very quarters on tier four.

138

Finally, he arrived at Brynn, who expected nothing lower than assignment to the first tier from her father's subordinate commander.

"Tier five," he said. "No room for thieves up here."

He exited the quarters with the two women assigned elsewhere and sealed the door on the remaining pair. Behind him, Coleman waited in restraint with the rest of the fifth-tier designees.

"You'll receive a district pass that corresponds to your tier. It is a sensitive item that must be carried on your person at all times and presented at every checkpoint. You may not ascend to a level above your tier without clearance. Understood?"

No response.

CPT Hernandez turned about and proceeded back toward the elevator. His remaining detail of guards ensured that the others followed.

The pressure and lack of oxygen in the atmosphere increased again as their lift descended to its deepest depth, condemning the party to the most severe section of the ship. They cleared through another checkpoint at the lift exit, recorded their photos and fingerprints, and were then released into a large open bay with guards at every corner.

"This is the courtyard," the commander told them, "where the passengers on the Fifth are stationed. The door on the left is where all males sleep. On the right, females. Lights out is at 2300." He directed them inside and closed the doors behind them.

The courtyard was a crowded chamber reminiscent of the storied prisoner-holding areas aboard cargo ships. The room itself was no larger than two high-school gymnasiums on the Beacon, yet there must have been at least a thousand people in residence.

Inside, the putrid smell of human waste contaminated what little breathable air there was—damage to the bottom of the ship had left the restrooms on this tier exposed to space and inaccessible. The passengers here were literally forced to live in their own filth.

Near the restroom entrance, the pair found the only available standing room, where the sound of air venting into space through the cracks in the damaged walls was clear. The rationed oxygen pumped down from the upper tiers was just enough to negate the effects of its expulsion from the ship and allow these passengers to breathe at all.

"Looks like we'll be on our own after lights out," Coleman said, laughing faintly and falsely as he spoke.

"I imagine they segregate the sleeping areas as a form of population control," she said, struggling to breathe under the smell. "Raising a child down here would be impossible."

"Have you looked around?" he replied. "There are no children on this ship. I haven't seen one anywhere."

"You won't find any either." A small man was eavesdropping just a few feet away. "There's no one under the age of fifteen aboard this ship. The Partition took care of that."

Brynn and Coleman stared at the man in silence.

"I can tell by your clothes that you're from the Beacon. I used to be a researcher there years ago and on 189 before that. My name is Anirban Acharya."

At that moment, the Fifth went completely dark, and passengers began clearing out of the courtyard.

"Looks like it's time to get going. Be safe. I'll see you later," Coleman said as he departed with the old man toward the male sleeping quarters. She watched them walk away for as long as she could before they both faded into the darkness at the other end of the tier. Then, she turned and followed the other women to their area, hoping for the chance to get some rest.

Personal space was unfortunately absent from the list of priorities during construction here. There were no beds nor furniture of any kind, and the women had to sit very close to one another to allow everyone inside. Brynn was appalled, aware of at least fifteen vacant rooms on the *Beacon of Hope* that were big enough for most of them to stay comfortably, away from the inhumane conditions of this tier.

But nothing could be done about it now. Her father would have some explaining to do if she ever made it out of here.

***

Most of the women in the quarters had just managed to fall asleep when an alarm sounded, summoning them to the courtyard. A team of guards gathered everyone on the tier for a daily population count—to ensure that those who belonged on the Fifth were actually there.

After roll call, a retinal scan was performed on each individual and checked against profiles in the ship's security database, as though there was any reason why passengers above would want to sneak down here or any way passengers here could ever get out.

When population count was complete, the guards brought in large boxes containing the food rations for the day.

Chaos broke out as the passengers rushed forward to grab anything they could. Brynn tried to spot Coleman somewhere in the crowd, but he was nowhere to be found. Even if she could find him, it was unlikely she'd be able to reach him. There were too many people here. The population density in this room was greater than that on the entire Beacon. Brynn opted to move away from the crowd and worry about food later. As she neared the back of the corridor, she felt a tug on her arm from behind and turned to find Anirban holding some food rations for her.

"Your friend told me you would try and skip breakfast," he explained. "Come, sit with me for a while."

She joined him in the same corner where they had briefly met the day before and opened the rations he had shared. The breakfast portion consisted of wheat snack bread and a packet of dry peanut butter that was unpleasant to eat at best. She was sure it would take her body longer than the time she had here to digest it, if she ever could at all.

"Tell me, are you close to your father? You remind me of him," Anirban said to Brynn's surprise. Evidently, Coleman hadn't managed to keep her story to himself.

"You know my father?" Less than one-hundred meters away, a man let out a hair-raising scream as he was beaten by another resident for his food rations. A small circle of empty space formed around them until the assailant stepped away from the man, leaving him in a seizure on the ground.

When the conflict settled, the circle closed, and surrounding passengers jumped at the opportunity to take anything else he had. Anirban continued, unaffected.

"Yes, your mother too. We worked together on 189 briefly. Incredibly stubborn, both of them. You and I have also met once before." Brynn looked up from her rations at his face, with no recollection of him whatsoever. "You were only a baby when they brought you here, so I don't expect you to remember."

"I haven't seen nor spoken to them much over the years. They've never told me about that."

"Well, they speak of you often."

Brynn wondered who this man was and whether he was legitimate or simply crazy. She didn't understand how it was possible for him to know anyone on the Beacon, let alone communicate with them. She decided to reserve her judgments at least until they had finished eating, owing him that courtesy since he had provided her first meal in a long time. The two ate their breakfast rations in silence, watching the guards do nothing about the chaos that continued its echo through the tier except drag away motionless bodies from the floor once it was over.

"Do you know why this colony exists and where it's going?"

"We're looking for a new planet to replace Corina-189," she responded, "somewhere we can settle down."

The old man's stoic expression toppled into a frown.

"That's what they teach you on the Beacon, but I don't think anyone with an understanding of the problem really believes that."

"Well, to be honest, it seems like we are planning on running forever," she said.

"What makes you think that?"

"The colony has traveled at least fifteen light years from the Impact Zone, passing right by three or four stars that might have had habitable planets. Why didn't we try to study them if we intended to settle down?

"That is a dangerous question to ask in this colony. Many of us are here on the Fifth because we fought for the same answer." Anirban sighed and glanced around the courtyard at the hundreds of miserable passengers on the tier.

"Come with me, child. There's something I'd like to show you."

Anirban rose slowly to his feet and led Brynn to the male sleeping quarters.

"Am I allowed to be in here?" she asked, cautiously following behind him while looking over her shoulder for approaching guards.

"They don't care where anyone is until lights out."

At the rear of the sleeping quarters was a vent hidden from view by a large cabinet, concealing a passageway that cut down at an angle.

"This vent goes down one level. Follow me, please." They entered and climbed down the vent until they reached an opening that fed into a large chamber at the very bottom of the ship. "We call this the Sixth. It's a level unknown to any of the ship's staff."

Instead of an area riddled with damage, waste, and overpopulation as she had expected beneath the fifth tier, she found an operations room that looked like it belonged on the *Beacon of Hope.*

"All throughout the colony are people just like you and me, people who don't want to keep running forever. To run is to betray those who died fighting for 189."

He pointed to the wall behind her, and she turned to find a portrait of the *Foundation*, with pictures of its crew taken just before Impact. They were all so young then but stood their ground when humanity needed them. As she looked at the image of her parents and stared into their eyes, she suddenly understood why she had been sent here. They wanted her to fight back too.

II

LOYALTY

General Hinds closely watched the UNIVAC 7000 in his quarters as it monitored the colony's status and direction. The 7000 was far more advanced than its predecessor, capable of tracking the positions and movements of celestial bodies within ten parsecs of the Alcubierre drive and enabling interstellar observation. He spent much of his time with this device studying the growth of (I) Elnath relative to the Colony's location in the Milky Way.

Today, like any other day, there was no significant change. (I) Elnath hadn't stopped expanding, nor was its growth slowing down. The infinite enemy continued across the universe, chasing them relentlessly through the void.

He turned away from the machine and found Lehman, who had entered without warning, sitting at his desk.

"Next time, ring the buzzer."

"I thought we were past that."

Hinds gave her a half smile and resumed his work on the UNIVAC.

"Anything new?" she asked.

"No, nothing significant. Though I'm concerned the Demon might be getting faster."

"Have you told the Council?"

"No. They'll only order us to speed up the drive, and that's no longer a feasible solution to the problem."

"Until we have a solution, I suggest you keep your concerns to yourself. You'll already need to answer to them for your daughter's actions. For now, let the Sixth do its job and figure something out."

"Is Brynn down there?"

"Yes. I've been in touch with Anirban."

"Good."

They stared at the machine together in silence, watching eternity ahead of them and oblivion behind, wondering to what extent the UNIVAC could be improved. Had they had the resources to enhance it, it might have shown them the entire observable universe and enabled humanity to find their escape, assuming escape was still possible. The drones they left behind seemed to have unlimited reproduction capacity, provided they could reach viable energy sources. And there was always the chance, however small, that in front of the fleet lay the same problem in another form. Perhaps in an infinite space, this story repeated itself, and more machines hostile to life waited ahead.

"I want you to take a look at something." Hinds walked back to his desk and pulled out a stack of binders containing decades-old personnel files. Among them was a picture of a woman both leaders knew very well—the former commander of the *Foundation*, Kelsey Cochran, posed in a maternity gown shortly after boarding the carrier.

"When was this? I thought the Council got rid of her."

"They did. This is a picture of her on the Mount."

He reflected on his old friend who had shouldered the near extinction of mankind—on her hands was the blood of many millions, including her own husband, the chief designer of the Dyson Sphere whom she turned against to bring them here. She had carried his child unbeknownst to her team during their final days on 189. The responsibility for so many shattered lives destroyed her mentally, leading the Council to declare her unfit for parenthood and command, separating her from both charges immediately after the baby's birth.

"Did she ever have the baby?"

"A little boy. Dean was his name, I think. He'd be about sixteen or seventeen years old now—and he's on his own."

"And Cochran?"

"Disappeared from the Mount after her breakdown. No one has seen her in years. Given what she had to endure, I don't blame her."

"We all made sacrifices back then. We all lost loved ones, but the rest of us weren't allowed to break like she did." She held his gaze without speaking and, for a split second, saw the young man she had broken all those years ago, here in this exact room. "What's so special about the boy?" she continued, focusing again on the present moment.

"He'll be useful in the days ahead. All we have to do is find him."

***

General Lehman's transport receded away from the Beacon during her weekly inspection of the fleet. She studied the ship from the outside, watching it carry the others as Atlas carried a planet on his shoulders, with the bubble generated from its warp drive. Off at a distance, the four other personnel vessels hovered in their usual formation, surrounded by dozens of smaller support craft that were fielded throughout their years-long journey.

She directed her loyal wife and pilot along their normal route out toward the forward surface of the bubble, arriving at their first objective twenty-five minutes after takeoff. They flew as close as they could to the energy field's curve, pushing against the strong tidal forces repelling their transport as the bubble contracted the space in front of it.

Ryan monitored her scanners, checking for any debris caught by the field. If it wasn't destroyed from inside, it would eventually become a projectile, obliterating anything ahead of them once they stopped. As was generally the case, they found none—asteroids and dust particles were thrown around the curve just the same, but that wasn't the sole purpose behind this maneuver. The energy-density field jammed inbound and outbound communications, enabling open conversation free of interception by the Council.

"Front-row seats," Ryan said. She transitioned the ship controls to the autopilot systems and propped her feet up against her console, watching the universe pass them by outside. "Easy to forget there's something chasing us, sitting here." She pointed out Bellatrix, Propus, and Menkar, stars shining brightly ahead, though distant from their ferry. Infinitely farther still, the Seven Sisters rippled through their surrounding nebula like the tides of an ocean. Anything beyond them was difficult to see. "What's on your mind, Paige?" The general was otherwise preoccupied, mentally as she often was, but Ryan knew she hadn't asked her to come along for no reason.

"Have you reconsidered joining the Sixth?"

"No, I haven't reconsidered it. I've had enough." Her disappointment echoed through the cockpit. Ryan's support had been requisitioned many times, always at the expense of her own wishes. She spent the better part of fifteen years a second-rate priority as the Sixth grew into Lehman's obsession. It seemed that every time they spoke, there was a new set of needs that only she could provide for the organization.

She felt Lehman's eyes on her without meeting them directly as she waited in vain for a different response. Her answer remained the same through the fifty-plus iterations of this discussion, but Lehman took the risk and pressed on.

"Do you remember our first flight together?"

"I do, but you wouldn't. You were unconscious. Do you remember why?"

She did, though she'd repressed the memory of Randall's Island long ago. Lehman tucked the thought away, along with her failed attempt at manipulation, and said nothing.

"Because you followed your friend and nearly died for it," she continued. "You followed him into Syracuse twice and nearly died for it. Now you're letting him walk you to your execution with this ridiculous idea of a coup."

"Sweetheart, we have no choice."

"You always have a choice. You just continue to choose him."

The bubble whisked away a cloud of dust in its path, tossing streaks of light around its shell and momentarily painting the cockpit a deep shade of blue. On the center console, an alarm sounded, warning them of their approaching time limit—a transport lingering at the bubble's edge for too long would raise concern at HQ.

"Ryan, everything I do is for you. I need you." Ryan looked back at her now, absent any sign of forgiveness or belief. She disengaged the autopilot systems, resumed control of the ship, and pivoted about, boosting their thrusters back through the center of the fleet.

She slowed to a drift for the final segment of the inspection and powered up the infrared beam atop the transport. Lehman shifted its lens toward receiving lenses on each carrier and fired the beam at intervals, confidentially signaling their captains to provide an updated count of their passengers loyal to the Sixth.

Her first target, the *Quaker Ridge*, fired back with two long bursts and one short. Two-hundred and fifty. Disappointing, but to no surprise, as the most conservative carrier in the fleet, solely responsible for staffing most of the Council Guard.

The Manhattan produced better results: four long bursts, up from two the previous week. *St. Robert* held at two with no meaningful change, and their capital ship, the *Mount Vernon*, gave them six. Six-hundred souls, plus the two new recruits the general had delivered herself. They were almost double their rival army but stood no chance in an open rebellion against the Council without significant coordination—there was work to be done, still.

The couple finished their journey in silence, docking at the Beacon against a backdrop of the increasingly apparent drones stalking the fleet. Ryan left for her quarters without a word nor a glance at her wife, and Lehman stood by her transport in the hangar bay alone.

***

The Council waited in the Beacon's court for the fleet commander to arrive, having directed him to this meeting once news of Brynn's latest crime was brought to their attention. All three of them sat at the bench towering above the courtroom floor, adorned with the antiquated ceremonial dress that presented them each with an air of false regality, though they were simply lawmakers and not monarchs. A jury of mid-level officers from the Council Guard filled the spectator boxes around the room, though this was an investigation, not a trial.

General Hinds arrived on his own and placed himself at the podium in the center of the room directly beneath the presiding official, Chancellor Harris, his former commander and the ranking member of the Council. She had not aged well, and the effects of some aggressive cancer ravaged her body far beyond its years. Karma, perhaps, for abandoning those under her charge at AO Baker. She was ruthless, entirely responsible for the Partition, which led to the deaths of hundreds of small children across the fleet. Next to her on either side were her props, the less-powerful members of her entourage, watching him with indifference.

"It's about time, General," Chancellor Harris said, straining through withered lungs. "Where is your deputy? I expected she'd be with you."

"She has a fleet to maintain, Chancellor, and I have one to command."

"I've not forgotten. We do appreciate your time, as I hope you'd appreciate ours, much of which we've spent establishing order and discipline aboard your ships." A sinister grin crept upon her face as the sliding door leading into the room closed behind the commander. On the screen behind her, she presented security footage from the vault a few days prior. "Now that you're here, you can explain this. Isn't that your daughter?"

He left the rhetorical question unanswered. This was not his first time down the red carpet on Brynn's behalf—the Council knew her well.

"A fleet of over one-hundred ships and ten-thousand personnel firmly under your charge, but it seems you can't even control your own daughter." Chancellor Harris was on her feet now, strengthened by the quiet laughter of her minions around the room.

"The situation is resolved, Chancellor. I've transferred her to the Mount until further notice—the bottom tier, a steep price to pay for a small mistake."

"You're out of chances, General. One more mistake from you or your daughter, and I'll have you both thrown out." A fit of coughing followed as she fell back into her seat. The laughing settled into a concerned silence for the three minutes it took her to recover. Another frequent occurrence, one that Hinds hoped each and every time would be her end. He scanned the courtroom—subconsciously measuring his chances of removing her from the picture, were he to rush the bench at this very moment. They weren't good, not yet, but he'd return one day soon with the odds in his favor.

***

Hinds met his deputy in the officer dining hall adjacent to the recreation block, where routine had found them on most mornings for the better part of the decade. Lehman made her way, tray in hand, toward his table at the opposite end of the room and passed him nothing more than a simple nod as she took her seat. They began their meals in silence until the servers at the food line cleared down their workstations and exited the dining hall.

Alone now with nothing but the faint hum of the carrier engines, she looked up at him and spoke.

"They'll be watching you now, you know that, right?"

"As expected." They briefly monitored the open space outside the ship from the ports at their section of the hall, watching for signs of surveillance at their location. With none apparent, Hinds shifted his attention to the ever-expanding impact zone staring back at them through the abyss and tracing its boundary with his eyes. The drones covered a vast majority of the night sky behind them, spread equidistant on all sides from what was once Elnath, save for a few hollow patches where they hadn't the energy nor the available resources to replicate.

They were running out of time. It wouldn't be long before passengers woke to the sound of machines at their doors, chomping away at anything they could use as fuel for their journey.

Tyrannical as she was, Chancellor Harris made all proposed defense strategies impossible, turning deaf ears to any recourse that might limit her already fleeting control. The Partition was the only attempt ever made to force her hand in an uprising no one expected to see here and hadn't seen since. It was crushed so relentlessly by the Council that the population never recovered in the years that followed. There was no more room for loss at that scale without results. The colony couldn't afford it.

"If they catch us, we're done," she said.

"I know. I won't let that happen." Both pushed aside their trays and leaned back in their booths, maintaining focus on one another with eyes as heavy as the weight on their shoulders.

"Have you found the boy?"

"Hernandez has a few leads. I need him on the Beacon."

"If he's still alive, that is. You'll be back on the red carpet the moment you bring him here."

Hinds reached into a bag on the seat next to him and retrieved a single document, placing it face-down in front of Lehman. "There is a way to get him here without raising alarm, but I'll need help from both of you." She turned it over and discovered an adoption request form—one of the very few ways for civilians to move between ships. "I've taken a lot from you and Ryan, and I'm sorry," he continued, "but I need you to consider it. He'll play a great role in all of this, as Kelsey did."

"She has no interest in helping you, and I can't make her."

"All I'm asking is for you to try, please."

She nodded faithfully, folded the document away, and left for her quarters.

He watched her walk away, knowing that this final request would likely be the catalyst, the nail in the coffin of her failing marriage. Ryan never wanted anything to do with the Sixth, protesting Lehman's involvement in the rebellion from the very beginning. She was content with life as it was, temporary as it may be, and Hinds denied her that. He had dragged Lehman endlessly into the fray and brought her down with them. But if she agreed this time, Hinds would have his ace, a decisive weapon for a one-way mission against the Council.

III

UNIFORM

The Sixth was quiet, with most of its usual occupants in retreat on the Fifth for nightly rations. Brynn sat alone on the tier, making initial preparations for an upcoming task, her first as part of her new team. She was to retrieve a blueprint tucked away deep inside an unfamiliar vault on the Beacon—one of a particle accelerator that Anirban himself had designed shortly before his exile to the Mount. Its existence was his transgression. The possibilities it opened for the colony to fight back against the Demon prompted Chancellor Harris to send him here indefinitely.

He had presented to the Council a plan to cut off the drones and break them away from their pursuit, allowing them a small window of a few years to establish a new home. It wouldn't have been permanent, just long enough to gather the knowledge and resources to cover the great distances that lay ahead at a faster, more efficient pace. Though initially receptive to the idea before the Partition, Chancellor Harris banned all research afterward into the strategy.

Anirban kept the details of the plan from Brynn, opting instead to spare her false hope—there were many, many problems to solve within the fleet before they could ever face the Demon.

The retrieval was impossible anyway. It was a heist she had already failed on her own terms as a resident of the Beacon. Every detail from start to finish was its own separate trial. An entire afternoon was spent on its development under the advice of a woman named Root, who claimed experience on a similar mission with her parents on 189.

Among her awards from that day was the prosthetic leg she used to hobble across the tier, greatly diminishing Brynn's confidence in success. Coleman fared relatively well with his assigned task, having been directed to pose as a Council guard, redirecting an intercepted shipment of weapons on the Beacon to the Mount. Though neither had the means to get back there.

Behind her, Coleman kicked open the vent leading onto the tier and descended its sliding ladder, throwing her rations on his way down.

"Where's Anirban?" she asked.

"Quarters, probably. He's been awake for a while. Save some of that for him."

She reserved the edible portions of her meal for the old man and kept the stiff packaged bread for herself.

"Couldn't sleep?"

"Not after the stories he told me. You wouldn't believe the scale of this thing. Even your parents are in on it." He sat across from her and tore into the first of two items he managed to salvage from the Fifth, both equally ghastly. If her parents were part of this, then the Sixth's ideology must have saturated the colony's government, at least at some level. *How had they kept this from her, and for how long?*

"They've pulled all the strings." Anirban climbed laboriously down the ladder, snapping Brynn out of a momentary trance. "Ever since the Partition, though you're too young to remember that."

"Is that what started this?" she asked.

"Yes. The only armed conflict in the colony's history. A young couple on the First took control of the bridge and launched an attack against the Council. Your mother went through great lengths to ensure you never knew."

"But why would she hide that?"

"Those were times of unimaginable horror. Some things are just better left unseen." He rummaged through the last remaining bundle of food that had been set aside for him and propped himself against the wall next to Brynn. "You asked earlier why there are no children aboard this carrier. It's because they were all killed, eaten by starving adults after the Council denied food rations to the Mount."

As though to underscore the heinous nature of what was just said, the Fifth and Sixth tiers went dark, ordering passengers to their quarters for lights out.

***

The sound of the alarm woke the tier after what seemed like only a few minutes. Brynn was ready and out the door with haste, her mind still charged with rage and confusion from the previous night. She had never felt betrayal until now. *How many leaders on the Beacon stood aside and allowed innocent children to be massacred?* She refused to be a bystander like them like her parents must have been back then. Today, she'd have her first opportunity to strike back at the Council and make them pay for what they did.

Root found her out on the main floor and pulled her over toward the entrance of the male quarters shortly after roll-call, where they waited with Coleman for the old man to arrive—he'd come up with a plan to get them back to their home ship. Anirban appeared sullen in the doorway from a second consecutive night without sleep, carrying a folded set of recently drafted schematics. He opened them out and away from the view of a guard standing at the center of the corridor, revealing detailed layouts of both the *Mount Vernon* and the *Beacon of Hope*.

"Listen to me very carefully. On the fourth tier, there's a maintenance bay where transports are taken for post-landing inspection. They're your only way off this ship undetected." He circled their objective on the level above and traced an arrow along the path they would need to take in order to reach it. "In about five minutes, the guards will conduct shift change behind the checkpoint at the entrance. When they do, run. Leave the floor and hug the left wall until you reach the staircase leading up. From there, it's on you. We need that equipment."

"Are you sure this route will take us there?" Brynn asked.

"Yes. I designed the carriers. Any last questions?" She remained silent. Her plans were rehearsed dozens of times through the night, playing over in her mind until all courses of action were well thought out. Brynn was sure that this time, she could get in and out of the vault without capture—and she'd send the blueprint back with Coleman's shipment. All they needed to do was escape the Mount, a task that none before them had ever completed.

"Go now. It's almost time." Anirban watched them leave together slowly toward the entryway, reminded of a different time when he'd entrusted two young soldiers with great responsibility, just the same.

***

Coleman slipped through first with Brynn close behind, holding tight to the left wall until it opened to a stairwell cut directly opposite the elevator shaft that had initially taken them there. No guards had followed them yet, though voices approached from just outside, indicating the start of their shift change. There wasn't much time—they would only have until roll-call before an alert was posted to the rest of the guards on the station, then two minutes for the follow-up count. After that, patrols would likely tear through the carrier and find them.

They ducked into a gap between the wall and the stairway, peering up at the railing above for oncoming foot traffic. Three guards descending from the Fourth, oblivious to the stowaways beneath. Both darted up the first flight the moment it was clear, rounding the banister on the next level toward their second waypoint: the air return leading to the engine room. Coleman took a knee underneath it and beckoned for Brynn to climb up.

With his support, she reached its cover, prying it away from the opening and wedging herself inside. The ensuing duct was tight, too small for her to turn around and pull him in, and too high off the ground for him to reach his own. She inched forward, searching for a space to rotate and go back for him, but found only a straight path ahead of her. Behind, she heard the vent cover snap back into place, and his footsteps recede down the adjacent hall. He was looking for another way.

Her only choice was to move forward, dragging herself stealthily along the passageway over a room of Mount personnel working below. She crawled along the endless tunnel alone, fighting against the hot air flowing through the vents until she reached a steel grate shut over her only possible exit. Immediately outside, massive lifts surged above to a higher tier and back down, carrying ships to what must be her next objective—the engine room.

Brynn laid still, unable to advance nor retreat the way she came, absent any sign of her friend as the minutes passed by without progress and without hope. She studied the transports descending from the lifts down to the platforms below, each bearing the unfamiliar identification tags of neighboring carriers. More and more ships came, lining the floor in order until the platforms were nearly filled. They cycled through a shack at the center of the room, spending only a short while under maintenance before being delivered to the docking bay. She realized that getting down would only be the first hurdle. She had to find a ship that would bring them back to the Beacon. Choose the wrong one, and all could be lost.

The grate bent slightly as she pushed against it one final time, though not enough to release her. Bolts on all four corners kept it secure, and there was no way through from this side. Brynn let out a sigh of contempt for her former self, who thought she might take down the Council. Her former self, who got caught and sent here in the first place. Her past decisions had killed her, leaving her to die alone in this vent.

Suddenly, a loud banging erupted directly underneath, shaking her out of despair and into panic—someone below knew she was here. Perhaps her movements had been tracked, or her last breath too loud. Without time to think, the bolts started to rotate one by one, loosening themselves from their holds. Then the grate fell, caught by the unknown assailant before it could crash to the ground. Brynn tried to make herself small and press down even further against the bottom of the vent but to no avail. The figure rose into view at the new opening, a Council guard, as expected.

Game over, she thought, before the guard removed his visor and Coleman, dressed in their adversary's attire, stared back at her. He pulled her out, and they fell together, tumbling onto the shifting floor below. The platform they occupied turned the final corner away from maintenance and jolted upwards a few feet from the ground in preparation for its ascent.

"Come on!" Coleman shouted, picking her up off the panel with moments to spare and rolling down to the next one in line. They were running now, out in the open and oblivious to everything around them except the ships ahead. Brynn concealed herself against a transport two panels ahead, frantically searching for anything relevant to the Beacon. Nothing.

Six panels forward, the shack churned out additional crafts, five of them unrecognizable. Then, at last, the final transport out of maintenance bore a call sign she knew, painted along its hull: *V-6B*, Versatile Six-Bravo—the deputy commander of the fleet.

***

"Ladies, good morning." CPT Hernandez saluted General Lehman and her wife as they passed through the docking bay and onto the first tier, exhausted from a night of tense negotiation. Ryan had agreed to the adoption, but not for Lehman and certainly not for Hinds. Kelsey Cochran, in her absence, brought her here to pay a debt incurred long ago, back when she had trained her as a pilot—that decision alone was responsible for her survival.

Ryan couldn't say no to her abandoned son.

"This way, please."

The halls of the Mount were emptied, its captain diligently ensuring there was no interference from the passengers of his own ship nor spies from the Council. Hernandez led them through the vacant corridors into the nearest elevator and down to the Third, the last floor where passengers held separate quarters. Ryan, slightly faint, steadied herself against her wife, who was unaffected by the change in oxygen levels as the doors opened and released them from the lift.

The search for Dean found him alone in a room previously thought to have been vented into space, at the back end of a hallway where cracks in the carrier's foundation substantially degraded conditions. Thick layers of ice were built up along the corners of the walls ahead, where inspections had ceased indefinitely, enabling the boy to hide here undetected for so long. His door lay next to a pile of rubble at waist height, remnants of an ancient conflict that had never been removed, lingering aboard the Mount as the effects of the Partition often did.

Hernandez approached the quarters and knocked twice, sure no one would answer. After a minute with no response, he retrieved a master key from his cargo pocket, opening the door to a room flooded with trash surrounding a small mattress with an unopened bag of rations on top of it, as though someone was lying there only a moment earlier. On the wall above was the same photo of CDR Cochran, pregnant with the evasive child that rallied them here.

"Dean, you can come out now. We're here to help you." Hernandez waited again with no reply, stepping forward over mounds of unidentified material, prepared to call out once more before one of them grabbed his shoulder and pulled him back to the entrance. Ryan had found him tucked away under debris near the door with a firearm pointed directly at them.

She stepped in front of the others in her group as they began to draw weapons from their own holsters. Dean maintained his posture, ready to shoot the first person to move toward him. His eyes were locked on General Lehman, who stared back with her hand tight on her hip.

"I know her," the boy said, his voice deeper than his small stature entailed. He rose from the trash heap, standing at just over five feet tall, still aimed down his sights at his visitors. "She was there when they took my mom."

Ryan looked back at her wife for an explanation she would not receive.

"Let me handle this," she told them. The others let go of their holsters and moved slowly back toward the door with arms raised. Lehman watched from inside its frame, her weapon drawn out of view. "I knew your mother. She was a close friend of mine."

"I don't believe you."

"Her name was Kelsey, and she saved us all." Dean's hand slipped away from the trigger-well as she stepped closer, recounting her friend and mentor. Ryan examined his face, gracefully thin—his mother's eyes looking back at her curiously, cautiously. She reached out and touched it, softly wiping away the small tear gliding down its surface. He lowered his weapon now, letting it fall to his side as she pulled him into her embrace.

"You don't have to be alone anymore." She held on tight, staring behind him at the portrait of her former commander, watching proudly from the wall above.

***

The platform carrying V6-B ascended through the tiers and positioned itself near the front of the docking bay, with its hidden passengers stowed away in the transport's storage compartment. The ship was second in line to leave the carrier, waiting still for its crew to board.

Brynn curled up inside a locker, tucked behind a stockpile of rations stacked in boxes along the closet interior. Across from her in a locker on the other side, Coleman stood wedged between fire-suppression systems. Both remained concealed entirely, skating through the pre-flight inspection on the first tier, thanks to the Mount's hangar crew and their complacency.

She covered her ears against the loud hiss of the transport doors opening to admit its boarding party at the front of the ship. Through a small window on the door leading into the cockpit, she watched her mother and her wife seat themselves at their consoles while a third passenger strapped himself in behind them. The equipment in the storage compartment quietly shook, rattling to the pressurization of the transport as it shifted forward on its platform one last time, ready for launch. They sat at the front of the line for departure, the hangar door ahead open to the adjacent fleet. Inside, the carrier's crew flashed a green light at the pilots, and V6-B was off.

The transport shot forward at an angle, darting away from the *Mount Vernon*. The supplies in its storage compartment pressed tightly against both stowaways until the craft leveled off outside, settling into autopilot on its way to the capital ship. Brynn leaned against the far side of her enclosure when the noise of the launch faded away, listening to the barely-audible conversation in the room beside.

"He's asleep, I think," she heard her mother say.

"This is probably the first time he's ever been comfortable." Both were quiet for a long while after—the familiar tension between the two clearly present, even through the ship walls. "Why did you take her away?"

"I had no choice."

"Another favor for Hinds?"

"No. An order from the Council." Then quiet again. Brynn struggled to maintain her balance as the transport adjusted its course to line up with the dock on the Beacon. "We were only captains then, pawns in the chancellor's game. Cochran was tagged as the mastermind behind the coup against her. True or not, it's what Harris believed, and she gave me the order to kill her. Me alone."

"Did you?"

"No. I transferred her off the Mount to keep her safe. Hinds doesn't know, the Council doesn't know, but now you do."

The transport slammed to a halt as it touched down aboard the Beacon and began controlled decompression. Brynn held her breath and steadied herself against the infinite silence that followed before the doors finally opened.

"Ryan, I've always done the best I could."

"Hopefully he believes you." Ryan knelt beside the boy to wake him gently, and both walked hand-in-hand out of the hangar. When they were gone, Lehman rose from her seat and made her way back to the storage compartment, standing in the doorway to inspect the room in its apparent emptiness. She retrieved a note from her back pocket and held it in the air, looking in Brynn's direction as though the walls before her had disappeared.

"Take this with you, and don't mess this up," was all she said before dropping the note on the floor and leaving the transport. The stowaways remained perfectly still, vulnerable, detected, and afraid to make a sound.

IV

TIME'S UP

"If you could see what I'm seeing right now, you'd be very concerned," the fleet commander said to Anirban over secure comms using the stolen radio in his quarters. Outside behind the ship, there were very few stars visible from the way they came. Darkness prevailed, expanding in all directions at an increasingly alarming rate and gaining on their position by the hour. Hinds scanned the fringes of the black ring on the 7000 and found the small but irrefutable movements of individual drones headed toward the colony.

Their time was almost up.

"I'm beyond the point of concern, General, with or without a visual. We've already failed. Nothing we could do will ever erase the damage already done. There are no more permanent solutions available, only temporary delays to buy us more time. Those, too, are fleeting."

"Can we at least break their pursuit?"

"That alone is my primary focus. We may be able to deny their progression along our route, at least for a short while, but we have to do it now before that route expires, and the open universe becomes our enemy."

The open universe. It was the hard place, opposite the rock at their backs. The space between galaxies they could not cross should they reach their own boundary. It was their destiny, the inevitable result of continuing to run from the problem they created. At the Milky Way's end was a void twenty-five thousand light years deep, the Great Wall between them and the nearest galaxy, Canis Major. Humanity would never make it that far, not as they were. Not at this speed.

"The Demon spreads like fire," Anirban continued, "the surrounding resources, its air. Stars, planets, asteroids, everything fuel for its growth. What happens to a fire without oxygen?"

"It's snuffed out."

"Exactly. No fuel, no expansion. I intend to suffocate (I) Elnath the same way—by annihilating all matter between us and the event horizon."

"The particle accelerator," Hinds said, almost at a whisper to himself. A familiar idea, one the old man had presented long ago. His plan was to deploy artificial black holes against the drones.

"As many as we can build. A daunting task, but we've done the impossible before."

"Just let me know what you need, and we'll do it."

"Right now, just a specific blueprint, confiscated by Chancellor Harris. Your daughter is already after it."

"Good. Keep me posted." He silenced the radio and placed it on his desk next to a folding picture frame with the three existing photos of his daughter on display. Hinds was only present in the first, standing next to Lehman with the crying infant in his arms as she reached for her mother. It was taken just weeks after boarding the carrier—even then, his record of attendance in Brynn's life was poor enough to warrant her unfamiliarity with him.

Her first day of pre-school was captured in the next image, where she held Ryan's hand by the entrance of the newly renovated education block, most of her face and her tears buried in the doll she carried—the same one thrown over the gate during the chaos of their evacuation from 189. The final frame presented a portrait of her at high-school graduation, one of two copies Brynn had left on his desk after she discovered the absence of both her parents at the ceremony.

Nearly two decades had passed since he first saw her rocking slowly atop her cradle, nearly two decades since he and Lehman risked everything to save her from the war outside. Time slipped away from him quickly and left him a stranger to his own daughter in the present day. He had missed everything, and there were no more opportunities for reconciliation.

Brynn had no chance of success at her current objective. The general's plan was deliberately built that way. The blueprint she sought was here in his desk, where it had been all along, hidden among the many plans kept in reserve after the Council tasked his younger self to destroy them. She would arrive at the vault to find nothing but the detail of Council guards that he recommended for its security, inevitably leading to her arrest and exile, as promised by the chancellor.

***

On the second floor of the Beacon, in a corridor seated directly beneath the bridge, guards readied their equipment for shift change. Men and women dressed in antiquated body armor and helmets painted black with the Council insignia at their centers—a silver fleur-de-lis. Their weapons were sourced from the same repository brought to the carrier at its inception, as was their limited ammunition supply. All they had left to project their authority across the fleet were the few thousand rounds unused during the Partition, and the Sixth planned to take all of it.

They formed en-masse with their chief at his post, calling off a manifest of numbers corresponding to each guard present. At the rear of the formation, hiding in plain sight, was Don Coleman, wearing the same uniform and armor he'd previously stolen on the Mount.

"Number sixteen," the chief read, waiting for a response from a woman in the second row.

"Present!" she shouted, trying to lift her voice above the taller guard in front of her. The chief continued down the line with every number in his detail until all were accounted for. Coleman looked down at his sleeve and found his own just as it was called from ahead.

"Thirty-three."

"Present!" He remained undetected by the guards around him, who should have heard a female voice from his number. The chief put away his manifest and delegated shift responsibilities, assigning the first two squads as roving patrols around the Beacon's vault and the last to transport duty, tasked with moving sensitive equipment between carriers. No one in the third group spoke to one another as their squad leader directed them toward crates of varying sizes piled haphazardly at the back of the room.

Coleman spotted his objective near the middle of the stack: a weapons crate filled with forty or fifty rifles standard to an era past, scheduled for delivery to the *Quaker Ridge*. He made for it as quickly as he could without drawing suspicion, following close behind roster number thirty-seven, who was headed in the same direction. They reached for it simultaneously, locking eyes beneath the visors on their helmets as they took hold of opposite ends.

"Could use some help with this one, Thirty-Three," he said, finally, abandoning the concern initially present on his face. Coleman nodded in agreement while silently assessing his odds at taking him down in a fight, should it come to that—he'd have to get rid of his new companion somehow.

The pair loaded their parcel onto a dolly stationed near the pile and pulled it away from the group toward a lift at the end of a hallway on the western end of the corridor. Their elevator took a full minute to reach hangar two, where a transport to Quaker awaited them. They shouldered the trip in silence, only broken by the occasional chatter from the radios clipped to their chests. Coleman glanced at Thirty-Seven, his nerves on edge as his partner stared back at him, keeping him in his focus as they exited onto the first floor. The fraudulent guard led the way, rounding a corner into the open bay, where the real one stopped him and lowered their crate. The hangar was empty, absent any other personnel or ships, and they stood alone.

"My wife," Thirty-Seven continued, "was the real Thirty-Three. Up until last night, when she came home without her weapon and armor." He clenched his fists and took a single step forward before an alarm sounded on their radios, calling all guards back to cordon the vault. Someone had been detained.

Thirty-Seven hesitated, then turned to run back to the lift as ordered. Coleman watched him leave and waited for the next transport to the Mount.

***

The commanding general and his deputy cut through the halls of the Beacon with Council guards in tow, following behind them in close stride as they reported to trial. It had come quickly. Chancellor Harris summoned them to her chambers less than an hour after her guards had responded to the vault. *Your daughter is in custody*, she had said menacingly, almost daring them to come and answer for her.

Court was already in session when they arrived, placing themselves as far as the guards would let them go. Brynn turned and looked over her shoulder at her father, standing ten feet away from her at the edge of the spectator box, with tears in her eyes as the Council listed the charges against her. The chancellor's minion read them off one by one, stacking her earliest juvenile offenses alongside her most recent crimes of theft. Hinds remained stoic, unable to reassure her without tipping off their adversary. Harris had waited for this, watching his every move and documenting every failure for this very moment, an opportunity to finally sideline her greatest threat.

"What say you, child?" the chancellor said once the list was complete. "How will you justify your actions? Or does your father need to speak for you?"

Brynn now faced the panel without a word—there was nothing she nor the general could say to absolve her.

"Step forward, Commander."

Harris pointed at Hinds, and all surrounding eyes in the crowd followed him as he moved forward next to his daughter and held the hand beneath her chains. Lehman joined them without being called and took Brynn's opposite hand. All three met the chancellor's gaze as she stared down at them, her usual ominous grin fixed upon her face.

"General Hinds, again, you stand before me on the red carpet for your failure, another of many over the course of your tenure. I'm beginning to doubt your capacity to lead this fleet. Perhaps I've allowed you to for too long."

"The colony is aware of our records, both yours and mine, Chancellor. The people remember who fought for them on 189, and they remember who ran away. They'll follow me regardless of whether or not you allow it."

"We'll see." She turned to address General Lehman. "I think it's fitting that you've brought your whole family with you to celebrate your promotion. Since you're all here, we'll do a ceremony before sentencing." Chancellor Harris rose to her feet, kept up by the remaining members on the panel. "General Hinds, kindly remove your rank and hand it to your deputy. You're hereby relieved of command."

He complied, tearing the four-star insignia from his shoulders and passing them to his counterpart, who placed them in her pockets and defiantly maintained her own three-star rank. The room fell silent as both parties challenged one another until another coughing fit sat the chancellor down.

"Brynhildr," she continued minutes later. "Onto the matter before us. No more warnings, no more chances. I sentence you to exile from the Beacon indefinitely for your repeated breach of good order. Effective immediately."

General Hinds pulled Brynn close. "We'll bring you home soon," he whispered before the Council guard came, escorting her by the chains around her neck to a transport, where she'd be taken off-ship to the prison she most feared.

"Help me, Papa!" she shouted, fighting back in vain against the army surrounding her. Here and now, there was nothing Hinds could do but watch them drag his daughter away, terrified and abandoned, knowing in his heart that this would be the last time he ever saw her.

V

DOWN, BUT NOT OUT

Brynn struggled against the weight of her chains to sit up as she regained consciousness on her first night of incarceration aboard the derelict cargo ship. It was the nightmare she had always envisioned, surrounded by dying passengers of varying ages, wasting away beneath the filth of those already dead. She could count the bones of an emaciated man sitting directly across from her, with eyes sunken so deep into their sockets that she wasn't sure if they were there at all. His companion, if they knew each other at all, lay next to him, skeletonized by the cannibals surely present on the ship. He stared back at her, absent the energy for words, taking only a partial breath before expiring in place. Brynn shifted her eyes away from the scene, undaunted, choosing to save her own energy and find a way out.

The room she occupied was a flat open space with a very low ceiling, too low for her to stand completely and smaller than her father's quarters on the Beacon. She strained her eyes in the darkness toward a steel archway situated next to her and braced herself against the wall for the journey to the abyss on its other side. A single movement taught her the effort required to survive here—the oxygen available was barely enough to sustain life, and she could travel only inches forward at a time.

Brynn dragged herself underneath the archway to the adjacent chamber, where the decomposed corpses of long-deceased prisoners were thrown together at the center of the room in a pile that reached the ceiling at its peak. There was no way around it without crawling over the bodies at its edge, and she stumbled reluctantly atop the first, then the second, before the chains around her feet caught an obstacle and threw her to the floor. She remained there for a long time, hours even, fighting to breathe what little air she could through the stench of death suspended around her.

Tears began their slow, familiar descent across her face as she surveyed the room—this was the end of the road. There were no additional paths save for the one she came through, no accessible vents where she could hide, and no secret way off of this ship. Brynn dug her hands deep into her pockets in a desperate effort to find something, anything to break her chains. Most were empty, cleared out by Council guards, but one inner pocket of her coat held an elusive hairpin and the note left behind by her mother.

"Your journey's not over yet. We're coming back for you," it read. On the bottom of the page, she found the letters "K.C." inscribed in bold print. At the same time, Brynn heard a soft cry echoing through the room, coming from the other side of the pile.

It's not real, she thought, forcing the hairpin through the locking mechanisms on her restraints.

There was a click as the pin found its mark, and her arms shot free from the weights restraining her to the ground. She pulled herself upright and along the bones at her side, searching for the only evidence of life anywhere near. Then, she found her, a woman groaning intermittently in the corner of the chamber, with her legs tucked underneath the half-eaten torso of another inmate. Brynn approached cautiously, unwilling to be the next victim of this well-fed anomaly—the sole survivor of the massacre that occurred in this room.

The woman's crying ceased as Brynn drew close, freezing in place only a few feet away. Even in darkness, her eyes shone through, fierce and crazed.

"I know you," Brynn whispered, her lips trembling as she spoke. Before her was a piece of history, a legendary figure often spoken about on the Beacon—Kelsey Cochran, humanity's savior. "I think my parents sent me here to give you this. They're coming back for you. For both of us." She retrieved the note again and held it at eye-level in front of her, silently praying for the safety of her arm as it was snatched away.

Kelsey studied it under the dim light, wiped away the tears from her face, and stood.

***

A sleepless night of planning brought the current and former fleet commander here, waiting across from one another on an elevator down to the Sixth. Their army was two-thousand strong at last count, two-to-one against the chancellor's guard with the odds in their favor. Brynn's arrest had taken them beyond the point of no return to their one and only option: ridding themselves of the Council forever. All it would take was a single rebel in the right place at the right time, and the struggle would be over. The operation was scheduled for the very next day when the chancellor would gather her henchmen to determine Hinds' fate and sentence him alongside his daughter.

They studied one another carefully, both aged from the previous day alone. The pain endured over a lifetime of contention was visible on their faces. Hinds passed her a soft smile in reassurance, though his own confidence in their success was steadily fading away. She returned it faithfully, and the weight of the world split in two.

"One chance to get this right," Lehman said.

"And we will." The lift opened to the fifth tier, cleared of guards by the Mount's loyal captain, and they proceeded together through the floor down the path created by its parting occupants. Absent the Council, they were nobility here—the colony's king and queen, approaching the regent eagerly awaiting them at the front of the crowd.

"It's been a long time, General." Anirban propped himself up as best he could on his cane and extended an unnecessary salute. Years had passed since they last spoke in person—ten since the old man's trial. A life spent investing in mankind's survival had earned him only a decade of despair on the Fifth, and he stood now a ghost of the man with the newspaper at the Terminal long ago. "I didn't expect to see you back here."

"There are some new developments I couldn't risk discussing over comms."

"Likewise. Do you have the blueprint?"

Hinds nodded and drew the folded document from his coat.

"Then come, I've found your solution." He led them to the entrance of the Sixth, with the crowd closing in behind them until they arrived at the vent and could go no further. Both generals followed him through the opening down to the operations center below and over to the 7000 at the center of the room, where a team of familiar faces gathered near the machine and its projections.

Around them, elements of the headquarters were divided into sections along the floor, each tasked against the organization's many remaining objectives. It was an elaborate setup closely resembling Central Terminal on 189, far beyond what either leader had envisioned from the Beacon. "Sir, ma'am, welcome to the Sixth."

Anirban took control of the 7000 and panned away from the image of the Mount until the entire fleet was in the frame. Projections of support transports detailed for the sustainment of each carrier were highlighted in red. One-hundred and fifty of them surrounded their host ships. At the absolute edge of the display, the Infinite Enemy maintained its approach, expanding ever closer as the minutes passed by—the eternal fires of hell, burning through the very fabric and structure of existence.

"Looks like time's almost up," Lehman said, tracing the small gap between themselves and the drones.

"We have a month, at best," Anirban said. "We've allowed them to grow undisturbed for almost twenty years, an eternity at the pace of machine-learning. The knowledge they've likely gained over the course of their expansion…inconceivable. But there remains one barrier they have yet to overcome: their resource requirement for self-replication. That is the weakness we'll exploit." He laid the blueprint flat, directly underneath the projection, and measured the dimensions of his old design.

"How many accelerators do we need?" Hinds asked.

"That's the wrong question, General. This solution is a one-way trip—how many personnel do you have on standby, willing to make it?" The room fell silent at his declaration, and all aboard the tier circled the 7000 for the response.

"Everyone here has made unimaginable sacrifices to get this far. I cannot order nor ask anything more of them. I only offer myself and any who choose to follow." He searched the room for volunteers and found none, not even the veterans among them who had fought alongside him on the battlefield many times. No one was ready to lose it all at the finish line, not after everything they had endured. "When the time comes, those we need will step forward, I'm sure of it. If not, we're all dead anyway."

Anirban nodded at his friend and continued, "For us to have the intended effect on our adversary, volunteers will need to carry the accelerators to their targets via transport and will never be able to return to the fleet."

He shifted the transports in the projection from their actual positions into a line stretching out to the rear edge of the bubble. Then, all available ships exited the drive in a staggered formation and activated their particle accelerators in a trail of drop zones extending millions of miles across. Behind them, the resulting black holes formed a gap in the approaching hive with drones at its center falling dormant, absent the fuel required to cross the immeasurable distance ahead.

Anirban sped the projection forward at four times the speed, and the drones on either end of the gap eventually pushed around it, encircled it from both sides, and resumed their conquest. "This plan won't stop them forever, but it will buy us time. A few years, perhaps, to build a real defense." He turned away from the 7000 to address his staff, standing in continued silence as the projection closed. "Three hundred souls, two per transport. That is the bill we must pay for others to live."

***

The fleet commanders provided an escort to the old man on his only trip above the Fifth since his arrival on the Mount as their lift ascended to the First. His health returned steadily as they rose through each tier, invigorating his lungs by the Third and his energy by the Second, allowing him to abandon his cane entirely. At the top level, he was his former self: the architect of victory—the leader the colony would need to survive in the absence of both generals, who knew deep down that they would not.

His initial bid for volunteers to shuttle payloads to designated targets delivered poor results. Their count held at two, returning only the names of the officers at his side as though there was another option for the personnel on the Sixth. There was no better way to sell this plan, no safer course of action available. This simply had to be done, whether they liked it or not.

"There's still the matter of development," he said, just as the lift slowed to a halt at its destination. "The Council will never give us the required materials nor let us use those ships."

Hinds looked over his shoulder without turning to face him completely. "The Council won't be around much longer. You'll have everything you need."

Anirban watched his children exit the lift together ahead of him, undeniably committed to the mission and silently to one another, as they were all those years ago. He watched them. Brave enough to jump into war from orbit but too afraid to admit their love for each other, even now. Both were still stubbornly defiant in the face of certain doom—neither having changed at all.

The trio made their way across the carrier's bridge into her commander's office, to the surprise of CPT Hernandez, who hadn't expected them off of the Fifth for quite some time. He sat at his desk, oblivious to their entry, staring through the adjacent porthole at a region of space opposite their direction of travel where stars had been previously but existed no more. The old man stood quietly near, joining him in transfixion at the oppressive distortion of the world outside. Darkness veiled most of the observable areas behind the fleet, leaving only a handful of galactic clusters visible, flickering as they too were eaten away.

"How beautiful it once was," Anirban said, his voice sour with anguish. The prison walls of the lower tiers had robbed him of his view of the surrounding universe, and he beheld it now, for the first time in more than a decade, as an empty shell. Their creation tore away at matter, nature, civilizations undiscovered, and stories unread. Humanity had destroyed everything, even the light that had filled the night sky. "We've already failed."

"Not yet," Hinds replied. "As long as this raft is afloat, we're able. We'll turn this around, somehow, for the rest of the galaxy." He sealed the door behind them and began a sketch of the Beacon's layout on a chalkboard Hernandez kept at the back of the room. It was a rudimentary drawing of the capital's top floor, left without detail until he reached the Council chambers and the hallway connecting it to the bridge. There he placed every corner, every turn, and every door leading into the corridor from memory, with the exact times it took him to cover each length during the trial.

Hinds circled the north end of the chamber and placed an 'X' atop the seat reserved for Chancellor Harris at the next hearing. "We're going to get rid of the Council," he said to an audience already in-tune with the decision—Harris was their chief contender and the sole barrier to success. "Tomorrow evening, she's scheduled to take the bench, where she'll sentence me to exile from the fleet. That's when we'll make our move."

He lowered his chalk and returned his attention to the team behind him, entirely stoic save for Hernandez, who remained skeptical and unsure about the risk.

"Sir, if we manage to reach her, every guard on the carrier will converge on us."

"I know. I'm counting on it. Once they're all together in one place, we'll kill them too." He traced the path running perpendicular to their target, which would serve as a funnel for the responding army in the minutes following the alarm, preventing escape from their counterattacking element. "Hernandez, I need you to assemble a militia of our best soldiers. Veterans from 189, if you can. I intend to wipe out their guards, down to the last man. As for the chancellor—" He locked eyes with General Lehman, seated beside the door with arms crossed in anticipation of the next impossible task. "Bring me Kelsey's son. It's time for him to join the fight."

VI

LET US DARE

General Lehman stood by the entrance of room 4-15 on the *Beacon of Hope*, staring at the pile of her wife's belongings stacked atop a cart near the door. Ryan was on her way out, hurriedly packing for transfer to a different quarters, one separate from Paige and her obligations to the Sixth. Dean's conscription that morning was a step too far down a path of immorality, their plan to sacrifice him too great a betrayal of his mother, who was still alive somewhere in the fleet. It had pushed Ryan over the edge, beyond the absolute limits of her patience toward her decision to leave.

She circled the space one final time and returned with the last remaining vestiges of their relationship. The photos that had lined the walls and shelves of the apartment. All that remained behind her was the furniture standard for each quarters and the few small items that Lehman acquired on her own. The rest was bare, forfeit the loving touch Ryan brought to their home.

"What will you say to her when she learns what you did to her son?" she asked, still irate from discovering their intentions. "What will you tell her about the boy she never had a chance to meet?"

"Ryan—"

"Don't. Don't you dare say you have no choice. He's a child!"

"He wants to do this to avenge his mother." Lehman forced herself to remain calm, though she instantly regretted the words that had just left her mouth. Any justification she gave now would only serve to provoke her wife further—her mind was already made up.

"He doesn't know his mother!" she screamed, nearly tossing the frame she carried as her hands flew above her head in exasperation.

And he never would, nor would he ever know she was still alive. The assault on the chancellor presented the significant challenge of reaching her chamber with weapons in hand. It was impossible. The same hallway that enabled the Sixth to trap their enemy also denied them the element of surprise. Harris and her posse would see any armed insurgents the moment they advanced. In a manner of poetic justice, Dean was volunteered to solve that problem: A young man who could walk in, under the radar, with an explosive vest strapped beneath his clothes.

Ryan wanted no part in it. She packed the last of her things onto the cart, and within seconds, she had abandoned their quarters, leaving Lehman curled up against the door, paralyzed, crying uncontrollably into her lap. The only woman she had ever loved was gone, another casualty in an endless war.

***

Dean Cochran waited impatiently across from the former fleet commander, flipping through the pages of a binder he was handed upon entering his quarters. He opened it up to the same photo that hung from the wall of his condemned room on the Mount, along with a few others that he had never seen, tucked within a pocket behind its cover. The binder was his mother's personnel file, containing records dating back to a time before the colony even existed. Inside he found an array of professional licenses she had attained and clippings of articles summarizing a bitter feud between her and the man responsible for designing the sphere.

Dean shuffled quickly through the seven or eight documents chronicling her existence to the last day she spent planet-side until he arrived at his own birth certificate and discovered the name of his father—the same man from the previous articles, though he left no signature acknowledging paternity. He shut the binder and pushed it aside, unmoved.

"She was a brave woman," Hinds said. "Without her, none of us would be here." The boy hesitated for a long while without speaking, focusing instead on the hologram projected on the other side of the room by the UNIVAC 7000. Suddenly, he got up and stood beside it, leaning in almost close enough to touch the display with his face.

"This is a map of the colony. Your mother commissioned these ships and damn near built them all herself." Hinds zoomed their perspective away from the center of the fleet until all five carriers were in view. The pursuing cloud was visible now, beginning its convergence on the bubble a little more than a light-month distant. Just as the old man predicted.

"Where is the Council?" he asked, with no concern for the approaching darkness. He had been promised an opportunity to strike back at the chancellor and take revenge for the hand he and his mother were dealt at the very beginning of his life, but the commander's plan had changed. He could not, in good conscience, sentence the boy to his death, knowing Kelsey would soon be rescued. Not with a daughter of his own.

"Young man, the path you want to take only has one ending. Whoever stands against the Council will have no off-ramp and no way out. That operation is suicide, and I won't send you."

Dean began to tremble softly, as though he wanted to run but couldn't. General Hinds was nothing more than another obstacle in his lifelong journey toward the resolution of his trial, and there was no longer any reason to be here. "They killed my mother."

"Your mother is alive. She'll be brought back to the Beacon once the chancellor is dead." Silence followed as Dean quickly struck away a tear from his cheek before it was spotted. "She's alive, and she'll need you with her," he continued.

The boy turned and bolted out of his chambers and back into the halls of the capital ship.

Hinds returned to his desk for the bottle of bourbon hidden away in its top drawer and poured the two glasses he knew he would need. He placed them both underneath the projection and took its controls, shifting the hologram's focal point to the fleet's rear flank and enhancing the image of the drones closest to the bubble. The largest of their ranks appeared on the display as individual units within the hive, machines as large as carrier ships, hosts to subordinate numbers unknown.

At the leftmost section of the area, he could see a single probe shot forward inches ahead of the rest and turned briefly toward the 7000's console, a horned beast staring back with the eyes of the devil at Hinds directly.

A hand on his shoulder brought the nightmare to an end, transforming the Demon back to its former image, and he found his friend beside him—fixated on the projection as though she had seen the same thing. He gave her the second glass, and they resumed their observation of the UNIVAC in silence, each waiting for the other to speak.

"She's gone," Lehman said, finally. She had crossed the length of the Beacon with tears still on her face, blind to surrounding personnel after her encounter with Ryan.

"Like the grass at our feet and the stars in the sky. How quickly we lost the things we took for granted." He finished his drink with a single pass, relishing the taste of smoky oak that took him home to Spectator's with Mcgregor, Ebon, and Jorge—all three pressing him to follow his heart and tell her everything. "It'll be okay. I won't be sending Dean. You can tell Ryan I'm doing this myself."

"What?" The room behind them fell as quiet and cold as the infinite universe outside. Hinds took her hands and squeezed them tight, burning her portrait deep into his memory one final time. Her presence alone had made him invincible, shielding him from the chaos of the world's end. She remained the brightest star in all of creation, a light so brilliant that not even the drones couldn't bury it. Not even death.

"I couldn't forgive myself if I sent anyone else. So I'll go on my own." A gentle cry replaced her words as he pulled her into a close embrace. "Paige Lehman, I love you. And I'm sorry I've never said it."

He wanted to hold her forever and follow her across eternity to the highest heights and deepest depths of the universe but knew he couldn't. He prayed she would stop him, tell him she loved him, and beg for him to stay, but knew she wouldn't. He wished for a different story, another timeline where he could spend his life with her, absent war and conflict, without pain and suffering, but he knew that would never be.

This was it, the end of the road for them, their last moment together.

Hinds took the chain from his neck and placed it around hers before reluctantly letting her go. She clasped her hands to its pendant, aware of what it was without looking. The single scar at its center an obvious tell. At that moment, she remembered laying helpless in a foxhole on Randall's Island, screaming through the dust and gunfire that flew overhead, struggling to reach Hinds as he stood against an advancing legion alone.

She felt the terror of the endless fall back to 189 and the enemy flak bursting all around them as it tore them away from one another over Syracuse. She saw him standing next to their baby girl in his quarters, staring down at the gold ring she now held beneath her fingers—the same one she returned to him years ago, on his worst day. She had loved him for a lifetime but still couldn't find the courage to say so.

"We have to go, Mama," he said, affectionately wiping away her tears before they reached her collar. "There isn't much time until the chancellor's in place."

She nodded, stepping back to present him his last salute.

"I'll see you around the campfire, Hinds."

"I'll be waiting for you there. Thank you, for everything."

They separated, with shattered hearts, for the last time as they approached their decisive battle. There was no one else who could do it. Hinds couldn't ask anything more of his soldiers, who had carried him on their shoulders for the better part of two decades. Nor his closest friend, who had sacrificed her own life for him, nor his daughter, who he had abandoned so many times.

He would pay this price on his own.

Hernandez monitored the *Beacon of Hope* from his seat on the Mount's bridge, hovering blissfully against the starscape at its bow. Ten transports surrounded the carrier in close formation, ferrying the two-hundred personnel chosen to engage the responding guards after the chancellor's death—a force large enough to combat the expected resistance without taxing the Sixth should they fail. Coleman's transport stood by at the front of the wedge as the lead element of the counterattack. His ship would touch down first and clear an entry for the rest of the unit.

In just a few minutes from now, a single blast would place the ranking members of the Sixth's opposition in one location simultaneously, as required by colony protocol in the event of an attack on the Council. Every guard on the Beacon would assemble on their chambers, condemning them to slaughter. In just a few minutes, the tranquility of the scene outside would transform into a frenzy of combat and confusion as the Sixth retook the fleet.

"Are the transports in position?" General Lehman entered the bridge without warning, and her appearance commanded the Mount's captain from his seat. The four-star rank crowned her shoulders and garrison cap as she walked alone to the center console. Hernandez and his entire staff looked back toward the foyer, conspicuously searching for any sign of the fleet commander, but found none. His replacement kept her eyes forward, ignoring their obvious concern—no one present was brave enough to press the issue or question it any further.

"Almost, ma'am. They're still en route to the staging area."

"Patch me into the forward element," she demanded. The captain directed a subordinate officer to establish comms with the lead ship, and a video feed of the cockpit on Coleman's transport opened on the carrier's main display.

"Their call sign is 'Versatile-Actual,'" Hernandez said. "The op commander is Don Coleman."

"Versatile-Actual, this is Versatile-Six. Do you read me?" she asked.

The pair waited a few seconds for a response that came in muffled but audible, slightly out of sync with the feed in front of them.

"Read you loud and clear, Six. Over." Coleman was confident, or at least he sounded that way, despite a complete lack of combat experience. Most of the soldiers assigned to him were survivors of the Partition who had escaped the chancellor's wrath and subsequent ejection from the fleet. Only a handful among them were veterans of the conflict on 189, but so too was the composition of their enemy.

"Actual, I need an update on your current status."

"No change, Six. Waiting on word from the ground before we step off."

"I want an update as soon as you make contact."

"Understood. Out." General Lehman closed the link, ceasing conversation on the bridge as personnel aboard resumed their observation of the transports outside, waiting painstakingly for the assault to begin. They wouldn't initiate their charge for the Beacon's hangar until Hinds made his move, detonating his vest beneath Chancellor Harris and her minions—Lehman would know he was gone as soon as the staging area was clear.

She kept the ships in focus for a long while, refusing to even blink, lest she miss the moment of his demise. Time enough passed for her to hope that perhaps he had changed his mind at the eleventh hour. Perhaps he had thought of a new plan at the very last second that would spare her the forthcoming despair.

This can't be, she thought. This couldn't be the way their story ended, not after everything they'd been through. There must be another way.

But there wasn't, and seconds later, Coleman dialed in, signaling his contact with their man on the ground.

"Versatile-Six, this is Versatile-Actual."

"Actual, this is Six. Send it."

"Six, we've made contact with Versatile X-Ray," Coleman said. Lehman sensed his confusion as he spoke through the static. "Did we switch volunteers?" X-Ray did not have the voice of the young man he had expected but rather the familiar voice of a leader he knew. Lehman hesitated, careful not to expose his identity over comms, before realizing it wouldn't matter much longer.

"Yes," she replied. "Versatile X-Ray is the fleet commander."

***

Hinds traversed the halls of the *Beacon of Hope* with five pounds of explosives strapped beneath his coat, taking the scenic route to the Council chambers on his final tour of the carrier. Sergeant Root had designed the vest herself, packing hundreds of nails along its interior fabric to ensure grievous injury to anyone caught in the blast. It was a lethal contraption that the chancellor and her minions would not escape, neither would the dregs of her personal guard, the fanatical remnants of Those For.

He passed by the recreation centers where Brynn had spent most of her childhood and imagined her here as a young girl, running through the middle of ongoing sporting events and competitions. He cut across the research facilities offset from the hangar bay and remembered experiencing fear for the very first time when his daughter was misplaced by her temporary caretakers, and he found her floating inside the micro-gravity chamber. The bridge was next ahead, with its lieutenants and specialists working tirelessly to keep the fleet aloft. At its center lay his seat and console, the throne from which he directed the last outpost of mankind, overseeing the colony and its inhabitants as they soared through the galaxy.

Concern for its occupancy once he was gone briefly crossed his mind, foolish as it was, given the current circumstances. It mattered no longer who his successor was. The mantle's porter would bear its weight just the same. In the event that they couldn't, Kelsey Cochran would recover from captivity and steer them onward. The puzzle was solved, and its pieces were in place—it was up to the others to extinguish the Demon and carry the fleet to safety.

A lifetime of war had brought him here as a man of no particular consequence, a soldier unknown to history and a martyr for the little that was left of humanity. His final act of defiance would earn him neither merit nor recognition, no mural, and no further reference to the battles won. The weight of his share would not grant him a seat at God's table. But it would give mankind a small chance, a renewed opportunity to turn the tide against an Infinite Enemy, and that was enough.

"Versatile-Actual, this is Versatile X-Ray," he said, speaking quietly into the stolen radio.

"Go ahead, X-Ray."

"Actual, I'm two minutes out. This is my final transmission. Take care of my daughter."

"Will do, sir. It's been an honor."

"Likewise. X-Ray signing off."

He took off one step at a time down the corridor leading into the Council chambers, with eyes fixed straight ahead to avoid seeing anything that might test his fortitude and slow his pace. He steadied himself and moved in small strides as though a single shift or bump in the wrong direction would detonate the explosives and destroy the carrier.

One minute and thirty seconds later, he arrived at the chamber doors and paused at the sight of his reflection, the lieutenant adorned with helmet and body armor, covered in the blood of his enemies from a recent engagement. Behind him, his family waited patiently for his soul to cross over and join them in paradise. He had lived without them for what felt like an eternity, longing for his mother's embrace, his baby brother's smile, and even the judgement of his father, who he knew would be disappointed in his effort. *You could have fought harder,* he would say, but there was nothing more Hinds could do.

With his affairs set in order, he took one final breath, placed his hands on the door, and rushed inside.

***

Alarms sounded immediately, directing guards on every level of the carrier to the Council chambers. They arrived within minutes, lining the single hallway at its entrance with weapons at high ready as their commanders inspected the scene. The room was nothing but char and ash, saturated by the smell of burning flesh from the unidentifiable bodies scattered throughout. Destroyed furniture was lodged into the walls at every side, hanging precariously above the ongoing investigation. At the court bench, the remnants of Chancellor Harris were laid flat against the podium, absent the vast majority of her upper body—the surviving half of her face stared down at the onlookers, still with its sinister smile.

Outside, the lead transport broke away from the staging area and docked at the closest available port on the Beacon, where Coleman's team dismounted to an empty hangar bay with no resistance from the responding guards, who were entirely focused on clearing civilians from the carrier's first level. They monitored activity between their location and the enemy formation at the end of the hall from an established perimeter facing away from the landing zone: disorder, as they expected, and counted on.

"This is Versatile-Actual to all Versatile elements, weapons-tight, commence landing." Coleman relayed the order through his helmet comms. The transports on standby acknowledged his directive in sequence and began their assault on the capital. Half the total force was on station right away, splitting into a forward element two platoons deep, with the remainder arriving minutes later as rear-side security for the advance. They initiated their push toward the objective hallway and its tenant guards, moving as a company-sized unit through a fatal funnel of their own: the narrow passage leading out of the hangar bay.

The Sixth crept through the exit at an idle pace, nearly trampling over one another as the front ranks lost their footing in full view of their adversary, the closest of whom lurked just ahead. Suddenly, a cluster of riot-control grenades exploded in the middle of Coleman's formation, engulfing personnel in a haze of tear gas and further impeding their progress. The Beacon's alarm sounded again, this time a single siren immediately above their position, shifting the attention of every guard on the floor toward them. Then the first shots rang out in confusion, from which side neither was sure.

"Get down!" Coleman shouted, dropping himself to the floor.

The few within earshot followed suit, narrowly avoiding the initial volley of gunfire that cut away the line of soldiers behind them. The haze thickened as the riot-control munitions rained down continuously on the scattered unit, erasing any semblance of cohesion. Coleman pulled himself toward the back of the formation, crawling over the bodies of his early casualties and underneath the bullets overhead, struggling to reach and redirect the security elements to the front. He found them lying prone, concealed by the smoke from the onslaught ahead, unwilling to stand and fight lest they meet the same fate as their companions.

Minutes went by with no break in the intensity of the enemy bombardment, and it seemed that with every passing moment, more guards had joined the assaulting ranks. It was only a matter of time before the cloud lifted and exposed the remaining soldiers to their doom—if they stayed here and did nothing, they would all be overrun. Out of options and fearing the worst, Coleman stood, indifferent to the storm around him, and demanded his army to take action.

"Fire back, or we're all dead!" he shouted, switching off the safety function on his own weapon. "If you have grenades, throw them as far forward as you can!" If nothing else, they would appear to be a larger force than they actually were and prevent their adversary from rushing forward.

He turned and began his charge, shooting through the smoke at random, oblivious to the rounds caught in his shoulder and leg. Behind him, his bravery was echoed by his soldiers, who rose to their feet and joined his advance, exhausting their ammunition with unrelenting synchrony. Then the fog cleared, and they faced the opposing force at point-blank range and one-third in number.

"Push!" he continued, determined to keep pace with the few rounds he had left. The turning point was fast approaching—the Council guard had nearly depleted their ammo stores as well, and both sides would soon be entrenched in hand-to-hand combat.

The last of the enemy rounds missed their mark and ricocheted along the walls into obscurity, then it was quiet, and only the sound of bayonets snapping into place resonated through the corridor. The Sixth darted forward with their knives drawn against their adversary, unarmed and untrained in the art of close-quarters battle, removed from the skill after years of disuse. The rebels of the Mount had learned to fight without weapons as a basic means of survival on the lower tiers, and that was their advantage. Massacre was imminent, as the guards ran in vain to the dead-end at the other side of the hall. Fifteen minutes saw them cut down to the last man by the handful of soldiers left standing with Coleman at the very end.

Behind them now, underneath the fading smog, were his casualties, strewn across the floor, one-hundred sixty personnel in total. Killed before retaking the carrier that had exiled them.

***

News reporters and camera crews littered the halls of the Beacon, trying to make sense of the carnage that had taken place just a few hours ago. Men, women, and children peeked out from inside their quarters, still afraid to exit, guarding their lives as though the conflict raged on. Government, for the moment, had disappeared, and the passengers aboard the carrier, immediately aware of its nonexistence, lost their certainty and comfort along with it.

No longer did the *Beacon of Hope* maintain the facade of luxury, or even safety for that matter. Their existence hung by the same thread as all the others, carried delicately along by the continued sacrifices of the colony's real leaders. General Lehman ignored them all, dragging herself through the scene arranged in front of her, impervious to the transients and their fragility—this was nothing compared to what she had already seen.

She passed near the remains of the court occupied by cameras in every corner and searched for others on the walls surrounding its entrance. Four of them lined the ceiling opposite the chamber doors, and at least one of them would have caught something, surely. Somewhere was a video recording of the Council's last moments and the ensuing slaughter—both of which she'd have to explain to Brynn.

She turned away and made for her quarters, unprepared for the inevitable solitude that would follow her arrival. Lehman stopped and leaned her head against the entry of 4-15, hesitant to face the ghosts inside, those of her best soldiers, of her wife and closest friend whom she had lost in a matter of days. Almost everything had been taken from her, but there was still more to do before she could rest. All that mattered now was the unspoken promise between her and Hinds that she would finish the fight in his absence. Even if she had to do it alone.

Lehman forced herself upright and pressed her key against the access panel next to her chambers, opening the door to the faint sound of the television she knew she had turned off before leaving the Beacon. Inside she found Ryan and Dean on the couch together, watching the broadcast of the day's events, and saw the video footage of Hinds rushing into the court and detonating his vest. The recording played over and over again as reporters from various stations pieced together the story of what happened.

"I'm sorry," Ryan said, throwing her arms around Lehman. "Paige, I'm so sorry for everything."

Both fell to the ground and wept.

VII

THE QUEEN

Brynn woke to the bitter smell of antiseptics commonly found in hospitals and med-stations throughout the fleet. She lay in bed, surrounded by large clinical displays monitoring data from various parts of her body, disoriented from her recent ordeal. Her experience aboard the cargo ship was difficult to recollect. The last thing she could piece together was the memory of Don Coleman carrying her out of the dark, airless chamber onto a transport, then everything went black.

She attempted to sit up and lean against the frame of the headboard behind her before a tremendous pain in her chest knocked her back down. The screen to her right sounded a quiet alert, flashing red around the corresponding area on the image of her torso.

"You're not going anywhere yet," a familiar voice said suddenly. Brynn turned to find her mother watching her from her seat across the room. "I'm sorry I didn't visit you sooner."

"Where are we?"

"We're in the med station on the First. You've been here a few days."

"How did I get here? I was just on the cargo ship."

"I sent your friend to come get you. You've missed quite a bit." General Lehman paused, unable to find the courage to tell her about her father. She turned toward the television hanging from the wall next to the bed, and both watched along in silence as the broadcast relayed a snippet of the devastation on the Beacon. To the general's relief, the reporters focused solely on the bloodshed outside the court rather than the reason behind it. After a few minutes, Brynn looked away and broke the silence. "Is the Council still after me?" she asked.

"You don't have to worry about them anymore."

"What do you mean?"

"They're no longer in charge."

"Then I need to get back to work on the Sixth," she said, successfully sitting up this time but still unable to lift herself out of bed.

"You need to stay here and recover. There's plenty of work to be done once you're well." Lehman bent over next to Brynn and kissed her on the forehead, paralyzing her with affection that she had rarely received, then departed the med-station for the Sixth before the girl had an opportunity to protest.

Brynn lay alone for a few hours, drifting in and out of sleep, wanting desperately to get up but unable to bear the pain. A week in confinement was worse than anything she'd ever been through, even her first time on the Fifth. She scanned the room again and searched for Ms. Cochran, wondering briefly if Coleman managed to get her out. The note had sent her into an almost catatonic state, and she threw it back in Brynn's face at the first mention of General Lehman, cursing her name loudly for leaving her there. She shook the thought of Kelsey from her mind and began to fall asleep again when the faint sound of an explosion drew her attention back to the news broadcast.

"We're still not sure how to describe what we're seeing here," a male reporter said. The clip flashed to a video of a man running through a set of doors before a powerful burst generated static on the recording lens. She recognized those doors from her trial as the entry to the Council Chambers but couldn't identify the individual charging through in her current state.

"But it seems that the chancellor and her associates have been assassinated by the former fleet commander," the reporter continued. "Stay tuned for further details as the situation develops."

It was her father.

Brynn forgot her pain and stood up, staring at the replay of the attack. She was broken, refusing to believe he would ever leave her like that. But how else could I be free? She watched over and over again, with tears in her eyes, as he hesitated at his final moment, blaming herself and her capture for his demise. Maybe if she was smarter, just a little bit faster, she never would have gotten caught in the first place, and he'd still be here.

She regretted every moment spent without him and wished she had tried harder to let him in. All of those nights when she turned out the lights in their quarters before he was home, she should have waited. She should have helped lift the weight from his shoulders rather than add to it with her behavior—she should have been a better child. Her entire life was spent thinking that he cared not for her, that his only concerns were his work and his fleet.

But there he was, sacrificing his own, discarding his chance at freedom, his right to see this battle to the end, and trading his share of victory for her.

***

Passengers scrambled between the tiers of the Mount, piecing together the particle accelerators for the decisive operation against (I) Elnath—the colony's final battle had begun. General Lehman converted the carrier into an operations center and staging area for the fleet of transports that would deliver their payloads. Volunteers from adjacent ships arrived en-masse after the attack on the Council, with no bureaucratic red tape nor barriers to stop them from traveling freely. There were more present than seats available on each chalk for the mission and far too many to count. Hinds' actions had lit a fire under them, leaving no excuse for cowardice.

Lehman combed the halls with Anirban at her side, assessing the crew's readiness as they worked on the remaining tiers. They had scrapped material from the Fifth and Sixth to assemble the components required for execution, dividing them among individual accelerator builds. Their pace was incredible, capable of potentially footing the bill in a matter of days if they could maintain it. If they even had that much time left at all.

"Everything looks good so far. Accelerator production is moving along much faster than anticipated," the old man said.

"How far are we from the first low-star density zone?"

"Less than a week of flight should take us there. We'll have two or three days before the bubble passes it."

"The Mount and its accelerator transport ships will leave the drive about halfway through," Lehman replied. Outside the ship, they saw the transports lined up to receive the devices that had already been built, though they were untested, as any activation within the bubble would destroy everything inside. So far, there were thirty ships, each prepared to carry one.

"Once we leave the bubble, there's no coming back. The colony will continue on at its current speed, and we will never be able to reach it again."

"Having second thoughts about coming with us?" she asked.

"Not at all, ma'am. I'll go wherever you need me."

"Good. Because I need you to stay behind."

"I beg your pardon?" Lehman stopped short of the bridge, out of earshot and away from personnel working on either end of the passageway. Anirban removed his glasses and cleaned them with his coat as though foggy lenses had clouded his hearing.

"I'm not letting you come with us, old man. Someone needs to run the colony." She crossed her arms and awaited his rebuttal, certain he would never abandon nearly twenty years of his life's work.

"With all due respect, I don't feel I'm qualified to do that," he replied.

"Your feelings are duly noted. As far as I see it, you're the most qualified. Unless you can show me another individual who has led every class of the population here and planet-side."

"The people won't listen to a poor old man like me."

"They will. And you'll have Commander Cochran once she recovers. Last I remember, you two made a good team."

Anirban nodded, seated his glasses over his eyes, and stared down the hallway past General Lehman at the hangar bay entrance. Behind them, Ryan stood alone at its archway, looking back in their direction.

"Someone's here to see you," he said. "I'll be on the Third if you're looking for me." Anirban propped himself against his cane and made his way to the first-floor lift, withdrawing himself to the lower tiers. Lehman met her wife halfway, unsure how she had found transport to the Mount with almost no ships remaining nor why she was here.

"I came to check on Brynn," Ryan said, aware of the concern on her face.

"You shouldn't have come. It may be a while before we can get you back to the Beacon." Ryan took a moment to shake off her dismissal, then placed the small bag she carried with her to the ground and smiled.

"Don't worry, I'm not going anywhere. I won't let you take any one-way trips by yourself."

Lehman had no words. Though this was her own last stand, the finality of the situation evaded her. She had almost forgotten that there would be no return for anyone left on this carrier—including herself. She looked away, silently plotting Ryan's exit and thinking of some way to change her mind. "What about Dean?" she asked.

"I left our apartment to him and his mother. He's there with her now. Kelsey is…well, she's better off than when she arrived. Happy, I think." She moved closer to adjust the collar on Lehman's uniform, folding it correctly behind her neck. Ryan placed her hands on her shoulders and met her eyes with determination and grit—she would not be sent home and left without her wife at the end of this journey.

She would rather die.

***

The bridge was quiet late that evening, as personnel aboard the Mount retired to quarters established on completed transports and in various sections of the upper tiers for their first opportunity at rest since the project's inception. The hall directly outside was filled with volunteers packed together on the makeshift beds they had created out of their few belongings arranged on the floor around them. Men and women of all classes, from all walks of life, in their final moments, sharing the same space and the same courage against a common enemy.

Lehman sat at the carrier's helm once again, mapping projections of transport staging areas on the center console, placing them exactly where they needed to be for execution in a few days' time. She felt the weight of Cochran's ancient words as she set the ships in a staggered formation from the very edge of the bubble to the Mount. It was her turn to ask others to sacrifice. It was her turn to order her loyal servants to their deaths, to relinquish their souls to the Creator who waited patiently with the billions already lost to this war.

In her lap was a familiar doll of a penguin wearing camouflage that she hadn't seen in many years. It was Brynn's favorite toy, one that would have sparked immediate concern had she left it with her at the med-station as planned. She didn't have the heart to upset the girl, after all she had been through, neither the resolve to drag her along into the abyss. Lehman knew that this doll represented the last moments with her daughter before she parted with Brynn and left her behind.

She studied the history of its voyage in its fraying ends when suddenly there was a disturbance in the crowd outside. They had risen from their sleep, parting to let a single figure through. It was Brynn, hobbling down the center of the tier with help from individuals on both sides as she struggled to stay upright. She fought her way to the main console and collapsed in Lehman's arms, right next to the doll that had served as her best friend from her earliest years.

"Hi, Mama," she said.

"Brynhildr. You're stubborn." She cradled her like an infant, hiding her tears and her anger at the sudden approach of her inevitable nightmare—she had hoped for at least an hour more before their final goodbye. "You need to rest. You shouldn't be here."

"I saw the news about the explosion."

"I'm sorry. We had no choice. The Council had to go."

"I know." She wiped her face, hardly conscious but very clearly hurt. She leaned forward, threw her arms around her mother, and buried her head in her chest. Lehman held her close and brushed her own face dry before Brynn could see. It was the same loss repeated of the family she would never again be able to reach.

"I heard the Mount will be leaving the bubble soon. Is that true?"

"Yes. We can't beat the Demon from inside."

Brynn nodded understanding without leaving the shelter of the general's lap. "I hope the colony finds a new home soon."

"Whether or not that happens is up to you. You'll be staying with them."

Lehman pushed the girl away just enough to raise her head and look at her, staring into the same beautiful eyes of the child she had rescued long ago. Brynn stared back, stoic as the day of their initial encounter, the Armored Fighting Woman for whom she was named. She was fully present now, startled and alert by the revelation, but silent still.

"I carried you in my arms for the first time on my hardest day, after a fight that nearly took everything from me. Your smile saved me back then, and I swore to myself that I'd do anything to protect you, my sweet baby, from trouble. I will not betray that decision nor your father in heaven by throwing your life away. I love you infinitely, and he loved you too. You're all we ever had." Lehman stood her up and handed her the doll, transferring her soul in the process, it seemed.

"That's not fair," she whimpered. "This is my fight too."

"You deserve to finish it." Tears fell down both of their faces as Lehman took her hand. "This isn't the end, but I'm charging you, Dr. Acharya, and Commander Cochran to get us there. Return to the Beacon and help them."

Brynn began to storm away angrily but stopped herself short of the exit and ran back to her mother's embrace—she would not lose another parent to contempt, even if they'd be lost for a third time to hostility.

"I love you, Mama," she cried, barely audible in her despair.

"I'll always watch over you, sweetheart. We both will. Don't let us down." Lehman reluctantly let her go and walked her to the archway leading out of the bridge toward the passage into the hangar bay. She called the floor to attention, ordering everyone in the hallway to their feet, and they stood without hesitation and faced them.

"Last call of service to the Sixth. Exiting, Brynn Hinds, end of tour." The general rendered a salute, and all present followed, holding their honors until her daughter was off the floor, standing in the hangar bay for the next available transport. Brynn turned to the bridge to see her mother one final time and found something she wasn't sure was real.

Across the tier, standing next to General Lehman, unbeknownst to her and everyone else, was the faint apparition of her father, standing at attention and presenting his salute to her as well.

VIII

DEPARTURE

The eve of battle brought an eerie atmosphere to the Mount. Fear and apprehension settled like a dense fog over each tier. It was the crew's final day, their last moments before departure from humanity's only remaining outpost, and their first direct exchange with (I) Elnath. Outside, the Demon made an approach so close that they could almost see it, with the largest of its drones stippling the view from the bubble's edge with their movements across space. The growth of each individual entity had exceeded requirements for the initial Dyson Sphere, and the speed of the flood far outpaced their own. Unhindered machine learning had advanced their enemy well beyond anything they could ever comprehend.

General Lehman monitored their inexorable progress from the UNIVAC 7000 in Hernandez's former quarters on the First, certain she could hear them roaring across the soundless expanse. She felt their malice, their hunger to devour eternity screaming loud above the voices of worlds and civilizations already consumed. All the Demon needed now was patience, the resolve to wait out a dormant expedition across the endless void, and they would win. With enough time, they would cover any gap, natural or manmade—they would destroy the universe, regardless of what happened here.

Still, there was no other option but to try. Lehman shifted the 7000's display to reflect the status of the fleet and the transports surrounding the carrier for launch, scanning each ship one by one for any last-minute faults that might jeopardize the operation. They were all low on fuel, owing their exhaustion to the resource cost of the drive's ignition fifteen years prior and incapable of long-distance travel. Any lack of precision during exit would leave the transports stranded, too far from their objectives to have a meaningful impact.

The target was a previously unmapped cluster of celestial objects with a density low enough that they could render it void using particle accelerator drops at one-hundred million mile intervals, leaving behind two transports every five minutes. The Mount would be the last to leave the colony, with the most powerful accelerator Anirban could fit within its hull, given his limited time constraints. Lehman only hoped the staggered deployment would create a buffer large enough to deter any further encroachment on the rest of mankind, wherever they ended their journey.

Had she understood the gravity of the trial before them, she might have volunteered herself for the attack on the Council, too—that was a simple task, the easy way out. Hinds would miss the real challenge, the contest of species organic and machine for continued existence. She wouldn't see it either, she supposed, as this was to be the first of many counters required of humanity for survival.

"One-hundred and fifty prepped and ready for departure with crews and devices onboard. Standing by for your orders." Lehman turned to find Anirban hunched against his cane behind her. "A single ship in the hangar bay to take Hernandez and I to the Beacon. Though there's still time for you to change your mind."

"I'm surprised you're still here, old man. My decision stands. You and Cochran have orchestrated victory from the beginning. It's only fair that you both see the battle to its close."

"Very well. There will be no comms between you and the colony, so I came to say goodbye and good luck, though we'll all meet again, someday." He shook her hand firmly in his, with the grip strength of someone one-third his age, and smiled. "It has been an incredible honor and privilege to make this journey with you. Both of you. Thank you for everything."

"Likewise, sir. Thank you for bringing us this far."

Anirban straightened out as he could and gave his final salute. "The four-star rank fits you well." He turned and made his way back toward the hangar bay, where CPT Hernandez waited to fly him off-ship.

It was her last goodbye, at least the last she could bear to make. She had no more tears left to cry, nothing left of her heart and soul to give up. Everything she cared for was returned unwillingly to the hands of God, and she stood in the face of humanity's greatest enemy as its champion, though she was but an empty shell. Lehman had made it further than she ever thought she could. If she couldn't bring them success now, it was never meant to be.

***

"We still have a little while before we're close enough to start," Ryan said. She sat with Lehman alone on the bridge, fixated on the comically large red button near the center console that would end it all for everyone left aboard the Mount in just a short while. The moment it was pressed, the accelerator would generate a black hole of unknown dimensions, fully absorbing the carrier and blocking the advance of any drone that approached along their target route. Lehman could sense her anxiety, her growing fear that at any second, they'd reach their destination, and the very last act of their play would be complete. "I think you made the right choice sending them back," Ryan continued, struggling admirably to hide the tremor in her voice.

"I'd have sent everyone back if I could. Including you."

"You're mistaken if you ever thought I'd let you do this on your own."

The two smiled at one another briefly and passed the next few minutes in silence, staring closely at one another before a notification from the 7000 woke them from their dreams. The fleet was nearing the first of its drop zones.

"It's time," Lehman said.

She broadcasted a video feed of the bridge from her console to displays posted throughout the carrier and on each transport in its surrounding formation. Her image towered over the remaining volunteers, the men and women seated in the staggered column near the bubble's edge, and those pouring out from their quarters waiting for their queen's final address. She hesitated, fighting away any trace of doubt in her words before she spoke them, forcing into herself the same confidence she hoped to give her passengers.

"Years ago, mankind made a mistake and released a plague into the universe," she began. "Our creation destroyed thousands of worlds on its path through the stars, including Corina-189, which many of you knew as home. Before us now is an opportunity to strike back at the Demon, to give it pause in its conquest, and uncertainty in its purpose. Now is our chance to stand firm and show the heavens above that humanity will not go quietly—we shall not be defeated." The feed erupted with noise as the personnel outside and on the tiers below celebrated her resolve. It was their chance to take control of their destiny, control they had lost at the inception of the sphere built around Elnath. That chance was all they needed to press forward, even if it was only into oblivion. "Thank you for your years of service, your dedication, and your sacrifice," she continued. "Those present today are the true heroes of mankind, and I'm proud to make my last stand with you." She saluted her viewers, who continued to chant her name loudly in the halls after the feed was cut, and gave the green-light signal directing the transports to begin their push.

The first pair of ships hovered to the rear boundary of the bubble and slipped through, transforming into thin streaks of light in the distance as they left the colony behind. The following hours saw a continued exodus of spacecraft illuminating the night sky outside the fleet and lighting a path in the darkness of the universe behind them. The sight was captivating, urgency aside, as their final battle was fought with beauty instead of the carnage they were used to.

Lehman transferred control of the carrier to her wife as they inched toward its own departure and waited by the console with her hand over the red button. Ahead of them, the last four transports passed through the rift one by one until the Mount was all that remained. There was no resistance from the bubble on the path to its back wall, no push repelling them away from destiny, as there usually was on the opposite side. They held the nose of the carrier only feet from its surface for one final look at the remnants of 189 before they were torn away and separated at an infinite distance from all they knew.

"Say the word, and I'll jump," Ryan said.

"Jump," Lehman replied.

The carrier slipped through the exit and came to a dead halt from near-light speeds, almost killing them instantly, as the carrier slammed into the invisible wall of gravity, pulling them into the star they had landed beside. The structure of the Mount was damaged as the violence of their drop ripped away the second and third tiers, throwing the volunteers previously below into open space.

"Ryan, pull away!" she screamed desperately, knowing there was no way to maneuver and nowhere for them to go.

"I can't! The controls aren't responding!"

The Mount continued its spin on a decaying path into the star, and the frame of the First bent inwards as they fell, breaking pieces of the bridge ceiling from their holds. Suddenly and without warning, debris that had broken away as they landed struck the Mount on its side, knocking Ryan into the adjacent hallway and flattening it.

"Ryan!" she cried, but her wife was gone. The collision left a gaping hole in the side of the carrier where the hallway had been, and Lehman hung with all her might from a beam wedged between her seat and the console, unable to reach the button. Escaping oxygen rushed past her into the void as the vacuum of space sucked everything around her out of the ship, taking her energy with it.

She closed her eyes as her fingers began to lose grip, waiting to join the others in failure and in death. This was the end of her story—and a new addition to the list of promises she couldn't keep.

"Paige, get up," a voice above her said. The general opened her eyes and found a bright light directly ahead of an unidentifiable figure, extending its hand to her as the ship fell apart. She let go of the beam and took it, immediately recognizing through touch whose it was.

"Hinds," she said.

The two floated in silence, and for just a moment, Lehman was free. The chaos around her was frozen as though time itself had stopped. Flying objects remained stationary, and the fires that burned hot near her body disappeared. Lieutenant Hinds was before her as she remembered him in their youth. The young man who had stood alone, in her defense, against an army.

"Finish the fight," he demanded.

"I can't," she replied, tears rolling slowly down her face. The apparition merely smiled, held her hand tight, and began to fade. As he vanished, Lehman could see through him, and she saw her objective only a few feet away. All she had to do was reach it.

"I love you, and I'm sorry I've never said it," she whispered to herself. Then, the suspension of chaos ended, and the destruction resumed. Hinds was gone once more, but her own energy had returned. She used every ounce of it to vault herself against the escaping oxygen and across the crumbling bridge.

Seconds later, she found herself at the particle accelerator, now with only moments, maybe even seconds, to spare before the rest of the ship was destroyed. As quickly as she could, she threw her weight on the button and completed her mission.

Her eyes were closed again, permanently, and everything went dark.

***

The last outpost of humanity sat motionless now, free for the first time from the bubble that had served as its ferry and its prison. The UNIVAC 7000's aboard the remaining ships sounded a quiet alert that indicated a match with a habitable world within reach of the fleet propulsion systems, a planet three away from its host star, four-billion miles from their greatest adversary. The Demon had been cut off, at least for a while, from their relentless pursuit. Mankind was once again left on its own, free to either make the same mistakes or change for the better. The sacrifice of a few brave individuals had given them one more chance to exist the right way.

From the bridge on the *Beacon of Hope*, Anirban sat with CDR Cochran, staring out at the radiant planet beneath them, and hoped that this opportunity, for which so many had sacrificed their lives, would not be their last.

FOR PAIGE, MY DEAR FRIEND

You may never see this, but I wanted to say thank you.

Thank you for finding me in the darkness and for pulling me away from it so many times. Thank you for always being the first to my rescue and the last by my side when all others had left. Thank you for standing with me against a hostile world.

Thank you for being my friend.

I love you, Paige.

Infinitely.

And I'm still here, as promised.

I hope we meet again next time around.

Made in the USA
Columbia, SC
28 November 2022

72051847R00138